LAUGH LINES

Other books by Holly Jacobs:

Pickup Lines
Lovehandles
Night Calls

LAUGH LINES

•

Holly Jacobs

AVALON BOOKS
NEW YORK

Published by Thomas Bouregy & Co., Inc.
160 Madison Avenue, New York, NY 10016

Library of Congress Cataloging-in-Publication Data

Jacobs, Holly, 1963–
    Laugh lines / Holly Jacobs.
        p.   cm.
    ISBN 978-0-8034-9814-3 (acid-free paper)
    I. Title.

PS3610.A35643L38   2007
813'.6—dc22
                                    2006033071

PRINTED IN THE UNITED STATES OF AMERICA
ON ACID-FREE PAPER
BY HADDON CRAFTSMEN, BLOOMSBURG, PENNSYLVANIA

This one's for Jacob, who has a great sense of
comedy . . . and who I'm praying never becomes
a stand-up comedian because I know
I'd be part of his act!

Thanks to everyone at Jr.'s Last Laugh Comedy Club
in Erie, PA for all the help . . . and all the laughs!

Chapter One
How to Be a Knock-Out

It was watching her.

Danielle Sinclair couldn't see its tiny eyes, but she was sure they were focused on her, waiting for her to slip from her precarious perch.

A mutant bug with a thousand legs and a voracious appetite for women.

No, not *women*.

For *a woman*.

Specifically, that killer-bug wanted to eat *her* for breakfast.

Dani could tell that it was a highly intelligent bug.

It knew eventually she'd have to climb off the toilet seat and make a break for the door. It was willing to wait because it wanted a piece of her.

1

She could see the headlines. They could even play off the fact it was May first. *May Day, May Day—Woman-Eating Killer-Bug Corners New CEO of Hamlin Texts in Gas Station Restroom.*

Being a CEO meant making tough decisions—though she hadn't officially started her new job. It looked like her first official decision would be, stay on the toilet and wait for someone to rescue her, or rescue herself.

Dani wasn't overly fond of being rescued—she liked to think of herself as an independent woman. She'd started college at seventeen, completed her four year education in three years. Since then she'd worked hard to climb the corporate ladder and make a name for herself.

Yes, she was an independent woman who'd never needed to be saved by anyone and she wasn't going to start now.

Summoning courage she hadn't realized she possessed and praying that her sensible heels were also strong ones, she jumped off the toilet lid and onto the killer-bug.

Crunch.

Ugh.

Shivers of disgust crept up and down her spine as she threw open the bathroom door, needing to get away from her well-flattened victim.

Thud.

The door connected with something other than

the wall behind it. Something a bit softer than a wall if she'd interpreted the *thud* correctly.

She was pretty sure it wasn't another killer-bug. Darn.

Could this day get any worse?

Dani didn't want to find out. This was enough *worse* for one day.

Because she was a woman who was good at multitasking, she scraped the bug guts off her shoe even as she pulled back the door and revealed that indeed it wasn't another giant, killer-bug, but rather a man pressed between the door and the gas station wall.

"I'm so sorry," she gushed.

Dani wasn't normally prone to gushing, but she figured slamming an innocent bystander between a wall and a door warranted more than a normal apology.

The man gave himself a small shake as he stepped away from the wall. "No problem. I caught the door with my hand rather than my face, so you didn't break my nose or anything."

She was thankful—not only because she hated the thought of injuring someone who was simply in the wrong place at the wrong time, but because breaking that particular nose would have been a crime. It sat squarely in the middle of a handsome face.

No, not just handsome.

It was a face saved from being beautiful by a very masculine, heavy bone structure. So, she'd just settle for calling him gorgeous, but the word didn't seem to describe him adequately.

He had dark brown hair that bordered on black. Oh, if she published romance novels instead of educational texts, she'd say something like, *he had sable hair and piercing blue eyes*. No. Not blue. Azure. Yeah, that sounded nice. Sable hair and azure eyes.

But since Hamlin published educational texts, she preferred clear and accurate descriptions— gorgeous, dark hair and blue eyes.

Gorgeous was accurate and necessary to her description.

She realized she was standing and staring at him, so she averted her eyes and let go of the door. It thudded back into its frame.

"Are you sure you're okay?" she asked.

"Yeah. What was the hurry?" He did a head-to-toe appraisal of her.

If she hadn't just done the same thing to him, she might be insulted, but she had, so she ignored his assessment and answered his question. "A bug."

His eyes snapped back to her face. "A bug?"

Dani could kick herself for admitting a bug had prompted her hasty exit, but kicking herself in her bug-gutted shoes wasn't an option. She was going to blame the uncharacteristic admission on the stress of her first day at a new job and the bug.

She tried to make it seem less girly by adding, "Not just any bug. No, this was a monster bug. A mutant bug. A killer-bug, even. It wanted me for lunch."

"It's a little early for lunch," he said with a grin . . . a grin that only made him look even better. And better than gorgeous was pretty darned good.

"Breakfast then." How long had it been since she'd traded inane quips with a man?

Better question . . . how long had it been since she'd gone on a date?

Too long if she was practically drooling over a stranger. Time to get out of here before she made an even bigger fool of herself.

She forced herself into business-mode. Professional, to the point. "Speaking of breakfast, I have a meeting and I'm going to be late. Again, I apologize for almost knocking you out."

He shrugged. "I'm fine. And your breakfast meeting is why I'm here. I'm a friend of Chris'. He said you had car problems and needed a ride."

She nodded slowly. "Yes."

"Well, I'm here to play your white knight and offer you a lift."

"I don't normally take rides from strangers," she said slowly.

"I'm not a stranger. I'm a friend of Chris'."

She laughed. So much for staying in professional-mode around him. "Oh, and Chris and I have known each other for all of," she glanced at her watch, "ten minutes."

He grinned. "Let's try this . . . Hi, I'm Luke Miller. I happen to be heading in your direction and can save you a lot of time if you'd like a ride."

Dani glanced at her watch. "I don't know."

He pulled his wallet out. "Here's my driver's license. Call someone at the office, give them my name, my license number and that way, if you don't turn up, they'll know who to send the cops to question."

She chuckled. "Of course, if I don't show up, it won't really matter to me who the cops question, I'll be dead in a ditch somewhere."

Chris, the mechanic, rounded the corner. "Oh, Luke, you found her."

"Yeah. She was battling bugs in your bathroom."

Chris looked embarrassed, but not as embarrassed as Dani felt at having her bug-phobia outed.

"Sorry about that, ma'am," he said. "We've had a bit of an infestation problem out here. I'll spray the room again."

"No problem. After all, I won. Of course, I almost knocked Mr. Miller out with the door."

"But I have quick reflexes and saved myself."

Chris looked a bit confused, but shrugged. "Anyway, Luke's going your way, if you want a ride. Otherwise, I'll call a cab for you."

"Mr. Miller already made the offer and was just verifying his identity."

"I can vouch for him," Chris said. "We've been poker buddies for years."

"And you and Ms. Sinclair are so close that of course she'll let you vouch for me?" Luke asked, repeating Dani's words.

Chris looked chagrined. "Sorry. I'll just go call that cab."

Dani shot Luke a dirty look, then smiled at the sweet mechanic. "Don't be sorry. It was kind of you to find me a ride and I've decided to take Mr. Miller up on his offer. Of course, if I don't show up to pick up my car, I hope you'll report him."

The mechanic grinned. "You can count on it."

"Thanks, Chris, for everything," Dani said.

"No problem. I'll get the car up on the computer and see what the problem is. I'll call you this afternoon with a report."

"I'm in meetings all day, but if you could just leave word with my assistant and I'll call you back as soon as I can."

"Sure thing."

Luke nodded at Chris. "See you tomorrow."

He turned to Dani. "Ready?"

She nodded.

He led her out to the parking lot and an autumn orange Vibe. Dani thought about her very sensible, very business-like dark blue BMW and sighed. She'd always thought she'd look good in something fun like this.

Or maybe some neon colored Volkswagen Beetle.

Dani settled herself in the seat and checked her watch again.

Luke turned on the car and the radio blared. *"Good morning, Erie. This is Punch and Judy on WLVH, where love is more than just a song. We're here to start your morning with a smile, and speaking of smiling we're hoping to see some of you at Chuckles on Thursday. We've agreed to host their open mic night. WLVH and Chuckles have teamed up and some of your favorite disc jockeys will be MCing over the next few weeks . . ."*

Luke clicked off the radio.

"About how long do you think it will take to get across town?" She was still trying to get a feel for the city. It had been years since she left home and had lived in Erie. Oh, she'd visited, but visiting wasn't the same as living in. The city had changed and grown dramatically. For instance, today she'd already learned that rush hour on Erie's Peach Street could be as harrowing as morning traffic had been in New York.

"How soon do you have to be at your meeting?"

"About fifteen minutes."

He shot her a grin. "Well, I guess it will take me less than that. Chris said your office is next to Koehler Square?"

She nodded.

"It's a straight shot down Peach and over a block."

She laughed. "You're a very easy going sort of guy, Luke Miller. And with the way this day has started, easy is just what the doctor ordered."

"What happened today, other than you got stranded at a service station and attacked by a bug?"

Luke wasn't going to let the bug thing go.

"A *killer-bug*," she corrected him. "If you don't add the *killer* part it just sounds silly."

He glanced her way. "Sorry. Attacked by a *killer*-bug."

He smiled again. It was the type of smile that had probably left countless women melting at his feet.

"That's better." She wasn't sure if she was congratulating his terminology or that smile.

She gave herself a mental shake. She had to

get over this lust-fest. She was starting a new, demanding job. She didn't have time for an infatuation or even a silly flirtation with a man.

Luke glanced at her, obviously waiting for something. An answer to his question.

But what was his question?

"Has your day been so bad you have to think about where to begin?"

Ah . . . he wanted to know what else had gone wrong this morning.

Anxious to think about something other than the weird affect Luke Miller was having on her, Dani launched into an abridged version of her morning from hell.

"Today is my first day at a new job and I wanted to make a great impression, so I bought a new suit, but got all dressed only to discover there's a rip in the hem. So I had to change, but that meant pulling the top over my already styled hair, which meant not only did I have to get redressed, but I had to redo my hair. And as I put the new shirt on, I smudged lipstick on it, so had to find another shirt. Anyway, by the time I got out the door, I was already running late. Then while I was on the I-90 the little check engine light came on. I think they should have something a little more specific on that light. I mean, does that mean, *check engine now, you're about to blow up*, or *check it in the next few months*?"

The words just spilled out. Dani wasn't usually someone to bombard a practical stranger like this. But it was better than ogling her white-knight.

Luke was chuckling, which made Dani grin in spite of how bad her day had started.

"Sounds like you've got a comedy routine going."

"Oh, yeah. A comedy of errors pretty much sums up my morning so far."

Although, right now, sitting next to Luke in the car, she felt as if her day was looking up.

"So, there was the check engine light?" he asked.

"And I got off at the next exit. The darned thing stalled twice, but I limped into the station and thought my problems were over. But I snagged my nylons and went to change them in the bathroom—"

"You carry extra nylons with you?"

Darn. She should have just stopped talking after she said got the car to the shop. But no. When she was younger she used to babble on and on when she was nervous. She had thought she had licked the problem.

Obviously she hadn't.

She'd like to think that it was starting a new job that had elevated her heart-rate and given her this warm rush. But she suspected it wasn't the job at all.

She glanced at Luke. He was being kind, listening to her babble and giving her a ride. So she wasn't going to bristle over his rather mocking you-carry-extra-nylons-with-you question.

"Of course, I carry extras," she said. "You never know when you'll need them, and like I said, I want to make a good first impression today. Holey nylons aren't apt to do that."

"Okay, so holey nylons. That's where I came into the story . . . killer-bugs in the bathroom, doors exploding open."

"Yes. I think you're up-to-speed." She smiled. "And now you know my life's history—"

"Your morning's history," he corrected.

She laughed. "Right. So what about you, Luke Miller? What do you do when you're not out rescuing damsels in distress?"

"I own Chuckles, a comedy club downtown. With your little morning-from-hell routine, you could have an act. Come by on a Thursday and try it out at an Open Mic Night."

"Open Mic Night?"

"The evening is dedicated to amateur comics. We're teaming up with one of the radio stations having their disc jockeys come in and host over the next few weeks. There's been a nice spike in the pre-sale tickets since the promotional ads started. You could try an act. The audience is generally very supportive."

"That's nice of you to suggest, but I don't know if my morning-from-hell would cut it as an act."

"So work on another bit to try," Luke said.

"I think it might be a little more difficult than that."

"Maybe," he admitted. "To be honest, I don't care if you ever get up on stage. That was just an enticement to get you to come down to the club."

Before Dani could digest that statement and respond, the car stopped and he said, "Here you go."

The two story brick building stood north of Koehler Square. Dani remembered the Koehler building from her youth. They'd manufactured beer there, once upon a time, but for years, the building had simply stood rotting, a shadow of what it had once been. Rebuilding it and turning it into an economic hub was just another sign of how Erie was reinventing itself.

Hamlin Texts had bought the small building just north of the complex. The brick exterior had ivy weaving its way up the walls. Old, stately. It was the perfect home for a textbook publisher.

Her job was to take that old, stately established feel of her company and move it into the twenty-first century.

Her company. The words sounded sweet. Maybe a bit terrifying. Either way, Hamlin was now her baby. It was up to her to prove that she wasn't too young to do the job.

She was here.

"That was quick," she said. She wasn't sure if her reluctance to get out of the car had to do with nerves about her new job, or had to do with a reluctance to leave this man.

"I could go around the block a couple of times if you'd like to make it take a little longer."

She laughed as she opened the door. "It's a tempting offer, but I hate to be late my first day. Thanks again for the lift, Mr. Miller."

"Luke. Call me Luke."

"Dani," she said. "It was great to meet you, Luke."

"Wait." He fished in his glove box and pulled out a couple tickets. "Here you go. Enough for you and your husband."

He was watching her intently and Dani realized that the husband comment was meant to be a question.

Normally, she would have avoided answering it—she didn't have the time or inclination for a relationship, or even a brief fling. But before her brain could give the command to stop, her mouth said, "I don't have a husband."

"Your boyfriend then?" he asked, a grin on his face.

"Nope," she said, smiling as well, even though she wasn't sure why.

"Well, if you are coming solo, come on Friday about six, and I'll make sure I have time to come sit with you . . . just so you don't feel lonely."

"Are you asking me out on a date?" she asked.

"If I was, would you say yes?"

"I'd say, see you on Friday at six." She laughed not because either of them had said anything all that funny, but because the thought of seeing Luke again made her feel a bit bubbly. "Thanks again."

"My pleasure, Dani. Really, it was my pleasure."

Dani waved goodbye and watched the orange Vibe zip down the street. She stared at the building with its perfectly manicured lawn and the sign that said, Hamlin Texts.

She was only twenty-eight. Twenty-nine in a month. She'd graduated high school early, finished college in just three years, and worked hard to prove herself. This was her reward.

This was her challenge.

Somehow she had to pull Hamlin, a company known for its stodgy, uninspired textbooks, into the twenty-first century. She had so many ideas, so many goals for both the company and for herself.

Dani felt a mixture of pride and terror as she walked up the stairs to the front door. She smiled as she stepped over the threshold.

This was it . . . the start of a new chapter in her life.

What she'd been working for.

Somehow she wasn't going to just meet expectations, she was going to exceed them.

From the Comedy Journals of Dani Sinclair:

So, there I was, standing on top of a toilet, watching the killer, mutant bug eyeing me as if I were some kind of fancy dessert. Yes, I was his chocolate eclair. So, I did what any modern, won't-play-the-damsel-in-distress, doesn't-need-a-white-knight would do . . . I jumped on him. Have you ever tried to get mutant killer-bug guts off heels? . . .

Chapter Two
Brothers? Oh, Brother!

"*This is WLVH, where love is more than just a song. And I'm Cassie Grant-Cooper, here a little early. I'm here to share your evening. The phone lines are open. We're starting our evening off with a request from Lou for Macy. 'She' from the Notting Hill soundtrack.*"

"Sherri, turn off that radio. Even if WLVH is sending people down to MC on Thursdays, you know how I feel about listening to nonstop love songs and people pattering about their love lives, or lack thereof."

Sherri didn't answer. Not that Luke was surprised. She never seemed to hear him if she didn't want to hear him.

17

It was a female thing.

Speaking of females, he wondered if Dani would show up tonight. He felt . . . nervous.

Okay, nervous wasn't a very manly word.

Tense.

Now, that was a bit more manly. He was just tense. But for the life of him, he couldn't figure out why he was so worked up over this woman.

It wasn't that he didn't date.

He dated.

A lot.

He dated a lot because he didn't want to be tied down to any one woman. The club was his first priority, and if a man dated a woman too long, she tended to think *she* should come first. Which is why Luke never dated anyone for more than a couple weeks.

So the fact that he hadn't been able to stop thinking about Dani Sinclair all week had nothing to do with this date being a novelty.

And it wasn't that she was the most beautiful woman he'd ever met. Why, when he met her she'd been scraping bug guts—*killer-bug* guts, he corrected himself with a smile—off her very sensible shoes even as she apologized for attacking him with the bathroom door.

Her navy business suit had been extremely tailored and she'd had on very little makeup. He couldn't even tell how long her hair really was because it had been in a professional looking twisty style that disguised its length.

No, Dani Sinclair wasn't exactly a sex-goddess in terms of her dress, or even her looks. So that couldn't be the reason he couldn't shake thoughts of her either.

She'd been intelligent and had a sense of humor, two very nice qualities, but not all that rare.

Yes, from what he knew of Dani, she was a rather ordinary woman.

An ordinary woman who'd crept into his thoughts all week. As a matter of fact, his first thought this morning had been that he'd see her tonight.

That wasn't like him.

Wasn't like him at all.

And the fact that he'd kept checking his watch wasn't like him either. After all, she wasn't late. It was only ten minutes to six, so if she showed up this minute, she'd be early.

"Hey, Luke, did you call and place that order?" Sherri, his bartender, called out.

"Yes."

"Well, it's not here."

He couldn't get ahead.

Every time he thought he had every possible problem addressed, something else cropped up.

"They said they'd get it here today," he muttered as he walked around the bar.

"They haven't."

"Hang on, I'll call."

He almost thanked Sherri for giving him something to think about, something to keep him busy. He didn't know what he'd do without her.

He dug out the number and picked up the phone.

"Hey, Kent, where's our order?" He half-listened as Kent hemmed and hawed . . . the other half of his attention was focused on the woman who'd just entered the club.

It couldn't be . . .

He stared, studying her.

She was about the right height. The right age.

Speaking of right, just about everything about the woman was right. Her hair was a rich, golden color and curled helter-skelter around her shoulders. She was wearing a tight pair of well-worn blue jeans and a plain little blue top . . . a plain little top that clung to all the right places and emphasized that her figure was anything but plain.

She was a knockout.

And she was also definitely Dani Sinclair.

"Hey, Kent, I've got to go. Just take care of it. If it's not here in an hour I'm going to be unhappy. Very, very unhappy."

He slammed the receiver into the cradle. And walked toward Dani. "You made it."

She glanced at her watch and smiled. "Right on time."

"Prompt. I like that in a woman."

"Me, too . . . not just in women, but in men," she said with a laugh.

"I hardly recognized you," he said. "You don't look like the very professional businesswoman I rescued."

She laughed. "Maybe I went a bit overboard with my professional-look on my first day, but I'm new, young and the boss. I wanted to present the right image."

Luke wasn't sure if it would be a compliment if he told her he liked this casual image better, so he just said, "Let's sit down. I saved us a good table. Nice view of the acts, but off the beaten trail. If you're in the comics' line of sight, you tend to become part of the routine."

He helped her into her seat, then sat down across from her. "So, how was your first week on the job?"

"You don't want to know." She gave a small, dramatic groan.

"That bad?" he asked.

She nodded.

"Do I sense another act—"

"Hi, can I get you and your guest something to drink, Luke?" Sherri interrupted. Since her job was behind the bar, not on the floor, Luke knew she was checking Dani out.

"I'll take the usual," he said, giving her a look of warning.

Sherri just grinned.

"I'll take an ice water with lemon, if that's okay," Dani said.

"Sure," Sherri said, as she walked back to the bar, but not before shooting another grin at Luke that said he didn't intimidate her in the least.

Women. They were mind-boggling.

He looked at the one particular woman seated across from him and realized that mind-boggling or not, there was something to be said for the gender.

"So, you're week?" he half asked.

"Really, you don't want to know. Personally I wish I could forget."

"So it didn't get better after the car problems and the bug?"

"Killer-bug," she corrected with a grin.

"Right. Otherwise it just sounds silly."

They both laughed at the shared joke, and he could see some of Dani's tension fade.

"So what happened?" he asked, wondering what could be worse than broken cars and killer bugs.

"I have no idea. It's just that everyone was so . . ." she paused.

"So?"

"I don't know. Maybe *nervous* is the word I'm looking for. I wanted to present a business-like image, something that would assure them that despite the fact I was young, I could handle being in charge of the company. My age was why the board hired me. Hamlin Texts needs to come into the new millennium. But I'm taking my time. I haven't made any changes, or even suggestions, and yet everyone acted like I was some usurper overthrowing the country and not just a new employee."

"I don't think the CEO qualifies as a mere employee," Luke pointed out.

"Sure they do. I have people to answer to and can get canned if I screw up. That makes me an employee."

"I guess I never thought about it like that." Right now he wasn't really thinking about Dani's employee status. He was thinking about her lips. He hadn't noticed the other day, but they were very full and kissable.

Not that he was going to kiss her.

It was their first date, after all. And since they were having dinner at Chuckles, Luke wasn't even sure it qualified as much of a date. No, he wasn't kissing her tonight, but he'd like to.

"Well, that's how I think of it, just another employee, doing my job. And I tried to get the staff to think of it like that as well, but didn't quite manage it."

"Why do you say that?" he asked, wondering if that was lipstick she had on, or just the natural color of her lips. They were pinkish, but not a fake pinkish color. Very natural. Either way, the color looked good on her.

"Everyone walked on eggshells around me."

"Bet that was painful," he joked, realizing how lame it sounded.

Obviously Dani realized as well, because she said, "Please tell me you're not one of the comics."

"They won't let me near the stage."

"It's a good thing if that was an example of your best joke."

"I can do better." When she gave him a small, doubtful frown he added, "But I'll wait and try later. Finish your story."

"That's about it. The week was just painfully awkward. I want to spend some time getting to know how things work, who's who and what's what before I try to shake things up. But I didn't need to shake at all . . . everyone was shaken all on their own. I have to confess, looking forward to this, to seeing you, got me through the week."

"Really?" If he were a chest-thumping, egotistical sort of guy, he'd be pounding away after her admission. Instead, he just sat a little straighter and smiled.

"Sure. A chance to go somewhere fun, a chance to let my hair down and be with someone who doesn't see me as a threat."

He didn't comment on the hair thing, but if he had it would have been something like, *you should let your hair down more often.* It looked soft and tempting.

He'd like to run his fingers through it and see if it was as soft as it looked.

And having that particular thought freaked him out.

After all, he wasn't the type of guy who rhapsodized about a woman's hair.

Or her lips.

What on earth had Dani Sinclair done to him?

"Excuse me, Luke." Sherri was standing just behind him.

"Yes?"

"It's about that order. There's been a mix-up."

"Can you just take care of it?" he asked. He didn't want to leave the table, to leave Dani.

"No. The driver's being unreasonable. And I—"

"I'll be right there." He turned to Dani. "You heard?"

"Yes. Duty calls. I do understand."

"I'll be back as soon as I can. Order something to eat and enjoy the show—it's about to start."

"No problem."

He hurried off.

Sherri was right, the driver was unreasonable. He'd brought twice what they'd ordered and had simply unloaded it all in the back and left.

Luke rolled up his shirt sleeves and carried cases in, not wanting to have them stolen, then hurried to make another call to Kent. He was feeling hot, sweaty and more than a bit put out at having his date interrupted.

Kent hemmed and hawed much like the first call of the evening, offering up all kinds of excuses.

"You listen to me . . ." Luke said. He didn't yell, but did lay out all his complaints. He realized he wasn't the distributor's biggest customer, but he was a good one . . . a good one who was prepared to take his business elsewhere.

As he argued, he couldn't help watching Dani. She was engrossed in the show, laughing at the appropriate times.

He just wanted to get off the phone and back to her. He wanted to watch her reactions close up. He wanted—

Suddenly a big guy—a jockish sort of guy, the type of guy who spends a couple hours a day at the gym—was standing at her side talking to her.

She got up and followed Mr. Jock to the door.

But Luke caught her giving the stage a wistful glance as she passed.

He knew she'd enjoyed what she'd seen of the show.

She walked by the bar and gave a little wave.

"Sorry. Call me later," she mouthed and held out a business card to him, a number scribbled in red pen on it.

Dani was leaving with another man and telling him to call her.

Who was the jock and why was Dani leaving with him?

Not that Luke could blame her. Spending half an hour wrestling with this delivery didn't make for a great date.

Maybe this was a sign that they weren't meant to go any further than one dead bug—and a washed-up date.

Yeah, it was probably for the best that things didn't work out. After all, he had a demanding business to run and she had a new job to see to.

Neither of them had time for anything more than a casual dinner.

Saying it was for the best, didn't stop him from watching her leave and wondering who Mr. Neanderthal was.

"Yes?" Dani snapped when poor Allie—her assistant—opened the door Monday morning.

"Sorry," she quickly added. She had been short tempered all weekend, but it wasn't Allie's fault.

Dani believed in placing blame where it belonged . . . which meant this time she placed it squarely on her brother Mart's shoulders.

Well, not just Mart. She also blamed her blabber-mouth sister-in-law, Connie, who'd told Mart of her car problems and her date.

When was anyone in her family going to decide she could take care of herself?

She was almost thirty. She ran a company. She'd spent years juggling a full-time job and grad school, and landed on a career fast-track. She was a success.

She was an experienced, successful woman.

Okay, so she'd had a couple romantic flops. Well, not just flops . . . they'd been belly-flops, the type that leave you gasping for breath and walking around in pain for a while.

But she was well past that pain, and she'd learned from the experiences. She'd grown and moved beyond those blips in her love life. But no amount of experience or success would convince the males in her family that she wasn't some fragile soul, and nothing she could say would ever alter the fact that she was still the family's baby.

Still, she couldn't believe that Mart had the

nerve to come down to the club and insist she leave her date, telling her that Connie needed her.

It turned out that the only thing Connie needed was a good kick in the behind for telling Mart about Dani's date. Unfortunately, Dani couldn't kick Connie's behind because she was in her seventh month of pregnancy.

So, Dani settled on being mad at Mart.

He was five years older and had always thought of himself as her protector. What he didn't understand was that she didn't need protected.

What on earth had made her think moving home to Erie, near him, was a good thing? She'd been so excited when she'd heard that Hamlin was scouting. A challenge, and a chance to come home. She'd been thrilled.

After Mart's big-brother, let-me-rescue-my-little-sister display, she was less than thrilled. A lot less than thrilled.

Brothers.

They were the bane of every self-respecting sister's existence.

Oh, Mart had pretended to be sorry and even apologized, but she knew the truth, he wasn't the least bit sorry.

And it didn't take long for him to start in on her about her date. He didn't quite buy the notion that Luke was a friend of Chris', so he was safe.

But worse, a lot worse, than dragging Dani

away from her date on the pretense that Connie needed her, was the fact that on Sunday, Mart—that tattletale—had called Florida and told her mother and father and she'd been forced to deal with a three-way phone call and lectures about riding with strangers.

Her head was still throbbing from that particular conversation.

"Miss Sinclair?" Allie asked again.

Dani gave herself a little mental shake. "Dani, remember? Call me Dani." She shot the woman what she hoped was an apologetic smile and said, "Sorry, I was thinking. What can I do for you."

"There's a man in the lobby who insists on seeing you, though he won't give me his name."

It was probably Mart.

Leave it to big brother to drag her away from a perfectly nice date, tattle to her parents, and then show up at work on Monday morning to terrorize not just her, but her staff.

She was going to go show him that his little sister had had enough of his heavy-handed tactics.

"Do you want me to deal with him?" Allie looked nervous.

Not that that was a surprise. Everyone at Hamlin looked nervous whenever Dani was around.

Just one more irritation. Brothers. Dates that flopped. Nervous staff.

"No. I'll take care of him myself, but thanks."

Dani got up and stormed into the outer office. She might not be able to soothe the staff and convince them she wasn't an orge, only time could do that, but Mart? He was about to learn that little sister wasn't going to stand for his interference. Oh, yes, he was going to get his comeuppance, once and for all.

She had no problem spotting him in the outer office where he stood, a big bouquet of flowers covering his face.

Not just big, huge.

"What do you think you're doing here?" Dani used her best CEO sort of voice. She was proud that she'd peppered the tone with just the right amount of annoyance and exasperation.

The flowers moved aside and instead of Mart's face, Luke's stared out at her from behind the bouquet.

"I come in peace."

All her tension evaporated at the sight of his smile. She laughed. "You do, eh? Ah, did I miss the war?"

"I thought, after I got called away Friday, you'd be annoyed. I'd have called you—"

Dani realized Allie had trailed her out to the

reception area and was hanging on Luke's every word. She interrupted him. "Come into my office, okay?"

Luke glanced at her assistant, then back at Dani. "Sure."

When they were safely inside, Dani shut the door and said, "You were saying?"

"I would have called this weekend, but it's crazy at the club, and I'm not just making excuses when I say I didn't have time until it was way too late at night. I didn't want to wake you."

"You could have woke me up," she surprised herself by saying. And she realized it was true, she wouldn't have minded a late night call from Luke.

"Yeah?" he said with a grin.

"Yeah." She held her hand out. "Would you like me to take these?"

"Sure." He handed them over and Dani almost staggered under the weight.

"You didn't have to bring me flowers."

"Sure I did. My mother taught me a thing or two about manners, though you wouldn't know it by the way I behaved Friday night. Flowers are for apologies."

"There was nothing to apologize for. If anything, I should be the one apologizing to you. I'm so sorry I ran out on you like that. At least you were called away because of business—I can relate to that. Me? I was called away by an over-protective big brother. My sister-in-law told him I was dating *a man who'd picked me up*, and he felt he had to ride to the rescue with some cocka-mamie story about my sister-in-law needing me."

As an afterthought she added, "She's seven months pregnant."

"That was your brother?" Luke grinned. "I wor-ried he was my competition, but I couldn't quite make that work out in my head. I might not know you well, I couldn't see you leaving a date with one man with another man. But just in case—"

"You brought flowers?" she asked, laughing.

"I thought they would impress you and if he was my competition, they might just give me an edge."

She grinned. "You don't need an edge. I liked what we had of our date . . . you didn't need to impress me with flowers. But thanks anyway. It was sweet." Dani grinned. "Especially consider-ing it wasn't the most auspicious of first dates."

"Feel brave enough to try a second one?" Before she could answer, he hastily added, "Somewhere other than my club?"

"You're on." And this time she was definitely not telling anyone in her family she was going out with Luke. That should take care of Mart's terminal case of big-brother-itis.

"How about Wednesday night? The club is very slow on Wednesdays and I can sneak away without feeling guilty."

Dani didn't even bother to check her planner. If she had something else Wednesday night, she'd reschedule it. "Sure."

"Pick you up at your place at six?"

"Could we make it six-thirty?" She'd stayed late every day since she started at Hamlin. Even six-thirty would be pushing it. But for a second date with Luke, she'd make it work.

She quickly jotted down her home address and handed it to Luke.

Their fingers brushed as he took the paper from her and Dani felt a small shiver creep down her back.

She'd shivered when she'd spotted that killer-bug, but it was nothing like this one . . . this shiver had more to do with a certain zing she hadn't experienced in far too long.

"Six-thirty it is then," he said.

He started out the door, stopped, then added, "Dani, I don't really have time for a serious relationship. I was too busy to call over the weekend, but I didn't plan to call this week either. I wasn't going to call you period. I planned to take last week's disaster as a sign. But I couldn't stay away. I just thought you should know."

"I don't have time either, and yet, I said yes."

"We're quite a pair," he said.

She laughed. "If nothing else, it should be interesting."

"See you Wednesday." For a moment, he stood in front of her, and she thought he was going to kiss her. And she was pretty sure she would have let him. But in the end, he sighed, pulled back and left the office with a small wave.

Dani walked over to the huge bouquet and inhaled deeply. Maybe she should have said no, but truth be told, Luke interested her more than any man had in a very long time.

Despite the circumstances, their first date had been memorable. This second date would probably be even better . . . at least it would be if she could keep big-brother from interrupting it.

From the Comedy Journals of Dani Sinclair:

Brothers? Oh, brother.

When I was younger my older brother was annoying because he worked at it. He'd flick my ears, pretended to spit at me, mock my clothing selections . . . Heck, my brother Mart even trailed me on my first high school date. That's right, he 'accidently' ended up at the same movie.

Years later, I learned my dad had paid him to see that show.

Maybe it's not just brothers . . . maybe it's all male relatives.

The men in my life don't trust me to find a man. So, maybe I've had a few disastrous relationships, from a boy who stood me up for the prom, to a failed engagement.

But I've learned my lesson . . . of course there could be more than one lesson to learn when it comes to men.

Chapter Three
Babies, Blind Dates and Bits . . . Oh, My

" . . . And then the doctor said that maybe our due-date was off, so he scheduled a sonogram. From the results he said Brutus—" Despite her annoyance with her brother and his wife, Dani laughed. The two of them played with odd nicknames for the baby, threatening that each was the one they were going to use. Dani prayed that Brutus was a joke, like the others. Brutus Sinclair? Ugh.

Her sister-in-law grinned. Obviously, making Dani laugh and forget she was mad was Connie's intent. "Brutus is due in about a month rather than two."

Connie said as she sat on the couch looking totally Madonna-ish on Tuesday evening.

Dani felt her annoyance crumble away, despite the fact she wanted to hold onto it a bit longer.

Even when Connie wasn't pregnant, it was hard to be put out with her. She was sweet. That bone-deep, glass-half-full, rose-colored glasses sort of sweetness that was impossible to ignore.

No one in the family ever pictured Mart walking down the aisle, but he'd practically run down it once he met Connie.

Connie was just too good to let slip away, he said.

Dani had to agree.

Her sister-in-law had been great for her big brother.

Unfortunately, Connie couldn't keep a secret, which is why Dani wasn't about to tell her about her date tomorrow night with Luke.

She smiled her most innocent I'm-not-thinking-about-a-date smile and said, "So, I'm going to be an aunt sooner than expected."

"Yes. Brutus is in a hurry to make an appearance I guess."

"Yeah," Mart said as he walked into the room. "He's a chip off the old block already."

"No, way," Dani said. "He'll be sweet and cuddly. You're just big and annoying."

"Still mad about last week?" he said, not looking overly apologetic.

"More than annoyed. I might have gotten over

you interrupting the date with your lame story, but siccing mom and dad on me? That was hitting below the belt."

"You were dating a perfect stranger." He sat next to his wife, his arm draping over her shoulder.

"Mart, perfect is always the goal. Finding the perfect man." He looked confused, so she settled for pointing out, "And aren't most dates a way for perfect strangers to get to know each other?" She turned to her sister-in-law. "Hey, Connie, tell me again how you and Mart met?" Dani asked in her best sugar-won't-melt-in-my-mouth innocent way.

"Oh, it was so romantic. I was on my way to the theater. I got off the bus and dropped my model of the new set for the play and figured I'd never get it back together when Mart showed up. I think I fell in love with him over that hot-glue gun."

"Really? You mean you let a *perfect stranger* glue with you?"

Connie didn't notice the sarcasm in Dani's tone, but Mart did. He glared at her as his wife continued, "I knew right from the moment I laid eyes on him that we were destined to be together. Unfortunately, it took a bit longer to convince him."

"Two strangers find they're perfect for each other as they fall in love over hot-glue. It's so romantic," Dani said with an exaggerated sigh. "But Mart, tell me again how is that any different than my date?"

"First, you haven't said anything about falling in love, just about dating this stranger. And secondly—mainly—the difference is I can take care of myself."

"And I can't?"

"I—" He sat looking confused, not sure what to say that wouldn't get him in trouble. "You don't have a good track record with men."

"Pardon?"

"First there was that Jason kid who stood you up—"

"That was high school, Mart."

"It was your prom. You were devastated."

"I got over it a long time ago."

"And how about Karl?" His voice was gentler than normal, as if even he knew he should tread carefully.

"I was a college senior who thought I'd found a forever sort of relationship. But I didn't. At the time it hurt, but looking back, getting out then was so much better than it would have been if we'd gone all the way."

All the way, between her and Karl, involved a trip to Vegas to elope. She'd been packed, ready to go . . . and Karl hadn't showed up.

Practically left at the altar.

But that was then, and this was now. She was older, wiser, and it was time to lay down the law, or else Erie would never be big enough for both her and her older brother. "Mart, there were other failed relationships. We've all had them. But I survived. I've grown up. I lived for five years on my own in L.A. and the last three in New York. I did just fine in both, thank you very much."

"Yes, but—"

"And you'll note I met Luke in a very public place for our date."

He glared at her. "But before that you'd ridden in a very private car with him."

"Both my office and the mechanic knew who I was with." She turned her attention back to her sister-in-law. "When Mart took you up to his office—this very private office—did you call anyone to let them know who you were with or where you were?"

"No," Connie said with a grin. "She's got you, Mart."

"You always take her side," he grumbled.

Dani had seen grown men cower at Mart's grumbling, but Connie just laughed and ran her hand across his forearm. "I can't help it you're wrong and she's right."

"I don't want to see you hurt again. I was worried," Mart said so softly that Dani almost didn't hear him.

"The fact you were worried is the reason I forgave you, and it's the reason why Dani will eventually forgive you as well. But I bet she'd prefer a bit of groveling before she does."

Mart sat up straight. "I don't grovel."

"Yes, you do. And it's good for your rather overbearing soul, sweetheart. Now, tell Dani you're sorry and that you'll stay out of her love-life in the future."

"She better not have a love-life."

"Mart . . ." Connie's tone had turned from teasing to warning.

Dani watched in amazement as her older, never-admit-you're-wrong brother said, "Sorry, squirt. I'll try and stay out of your dating in the future. On one condition. There's this guy at the firm I want you to meet."

"Mart," both women said in unison.

"Dani, I owe you an apology as well," Connie said, shooting Mart a hard glare. Oh, it was rather akin to a kitten glaring at a lion, but she was trying and Dani appreciated the support.

"I thought your meeting Luke was so romantic," Connie continued, "and never figured my overreacting husband would interrupt it."

"Uh, you know, Connie, he owes me an apology for tattling to Mom and Dad," Dani said, smiling broadly at her brother. Her parents had never been able to handle him as well as Connie could and Dani was definitely enjoying his discomfort.

"That's right you do owe her an apology for telling your parents, Mart. I mean really, what if she'd caught us fooling around before we married and told your parents? I'd have been mortified."

"I didn't tell them she was fooling around—" He stopped short and stared at her a moment. "You're not, right Dani?"

She shrugged her shoulders, not willing to admit that it had been so long since she fooled around with anyone that she doubted she remembered how.

Wanting that groveling, she said, "You did tell them about the date and painted it in the worst possible light."

"Mart?" Connie said, warning in her voice.

Not even putting up a fight this time, he simply sighed and said, "Sorry."

"That wasn't the most impressive groveling I've ever seen, but it will do. You're forgiven. Mainly because you're about to make me an aunt." Finding out she was going to be an aunt had been the driving force behind Dani's return to Erie. Oh, she'd flirted with the idea of coming home for years, but Brutus was the final push.

Mart reached across the couch and laid his hand possessively on Connie's rounded stomach.

"Yeah I am making you an aunt," he said with such pride that anyone listening to him would think he was the first man ever to father a baby.

He looked at Connie and whatever left over annoyance Dani felt toward him melted.

The two of them were absolute crazy for each other, even after two years of marriage. Dani envied them their relationship. That's what she wanted someday—when she had time for a real relationship. She wanted that kind of love.

"Listen, I've got to get going," she said, suddenly feeling like an interloper. Mart and Connie were completely wrapped up in each other. "I'll stop by next week."

"Hey, we're having some friends over tomorrow, if you want to stop by."

"Sorry, I've got plans," Dani said. And there was no way wild horses could drag her plans out of her. Why, she could just imagine what new torture Mart would come up with. Never mind, she wasn't going imagine them.

"A date?" Mart asked.

Connie slugged his shoulder, not hard, but enough to make him say, "Hey, what's that for?"

"You're staying out of her love-life, remember?"

"It's not like I was going to go break it up if it was a date, I was just wondering."

"Well, don't wonder, don't think about it and absolutely, don't break it up," Connie warned.

"Fine, I won't, but I want you to meet my buddy Sam for drinks. I'll set it up for Friday after work. There's a bar two blocks from your office. Chauncy's."

"Mart," Dani said. She knew there was exasperation in her voice because that's how she felt. Totally, and completely exasperated.

"If you meet him, I won't tail you tomorrow," Mart said.

Connie slugged him again, but he ignored her and concentrated on Dani. "What do you say?"

"Fine."

"Tie that red scarf thing Connie got you for Christmas on your purse. I'll have him there Friday at six. I swear I won't try to break up your date tomorrow. But you call me if you need anything. Anything at all. And if you do happen to go out on a date, take your cell phone and call 911 if something happens. Right after you call me, that is."

"Mart," Connie and Dani said in unison.

"What? I wasn't interfering, just wanting her to be safe. And Sam, from the office is nice and safe."

"Dani, run now, flee while you're still able. I'll restrain the big, overbearing, nosy brute."

"Thanks, Connie."

The next day, Dani sat in her office, doodling in a notebook.

Brothers. You can't live with them . . . can't live with them.

Dani sighed. That wasn't very funny.

She'd been stewing over Mart ever since he'd broken up her date with Luke. It had moved beyond stewing to boiling over him after she'd gone over last night. She started to scribble notes to herself on funny Mart stories that might work as part of her routine.

Routine.

A comedy routine.

Not that she'd ever use it. It probably wouldn't be a good corporate image, having a comedian for a CEO. Hamlin Texts was a very serious sort of company.

She looked around her very serious office. Wood paneled walls, dark furniture. Serious.

Her predecessor was pushing eighty when he left. The office reflected that.

She was going to make her mark on it sometime soon. Redecorate, lighten it up, when she had time.

Speaking of time, she didn't have any to spare on playing with a comedy routine she'd never use.

She could just imagine her family's response if they found out she was even toying with the idea.

My mother and father were so strict . . .

She couldn't think of a funny description of

her parents strictness. Maybe strict wasn't a good word . . . goal-oriented. That was better.

Her parents had goals for themselves and goals for their children. Which is why Dani was where she was, doing what she was doing. Her parents pushed her away from studying drama in college and pushed her toward business. And in the end, Dani had been glad for the push . . . she loved her job.

And despite the distance, over the years her mother had become one of her best friends. But rather than reminiscing about the past, she got back to trying to think of a routine. Obviously bad jokes weren't the way to go.

Besides watching the acts at Chuckles the other night, she realized that jokes weren't really part of a comedian's repertoire. It was more stories delivered with just the right *umph* that made people laugh. Stories of family, stories of work . . . just about anything that had to do with the comedian's slightly skewed view-of-the-world.

All the comedians seemed to have a hook.

Dani needed something, some subject to make her focal point. Some hook of her own, an area of life that she could build an act around.

What did she know?

Family.

No. She didn't like using her family as comic

fodder, although having a big brother like Mart could be an act all in itself.

Single-girl looking for Mr. Right?

Okay, she wasn't looking very hard . . . hey, maybe that could be her hook. How she wasn't looking for a man and kept stumbling across them anyway.

She thought about meeting Luke . . .

I'm single and I'll confess, I'm not actively looking for a guy, but I do tend to stumble across some in the oddest places. Why, just the other day I was standing on a gas station toilet when a tall, dark, handsome man . . . Wait, you want to know why I was standing on a toilet? It probably had something to do with the bug on the floor. Actually, it wasn't just a bug, it was a mutant, killer-bug. If you don't say the killer-bug part, my being on a toilet to escape it just sounds silly. Anyway, there it was, eyeing me up for dinner. Being an independent, new millennium woman, I decided to jump from my safe perch and squash the slithery looking thing . . . that's when I stumbled on Mister-Maybe-Something-Special . . .

She chuckled. Yeah, it was rough, but something like this could work.

"Ms. Sinclair?" Allie asked as she poked her head in the office.

"Dani, remember?" She scribbled another

couple lines, not wanting to loose her train of thought.

"Dani," Allie corrected herself. "You asked me to remind you at five-thirty that you had to leave on time today."

"It's five-thirty already?" Dani shut the note-book she was writing in. "Thanks. I've got a date . . . one I don't want to be late for."

"The flower man?" Allie asked.

"Yes," Dani admitted. The huge arrangement brightened up the cabinet across from her desk. Every time she looked at the flowers, she thought of Luke.

"He seemed nice. It's been a long time since I met a nice guy," Allie said with a sigh. "The men here at Hamlin are either married or too old. Even if they weren't, office romances aren't ever a good idea. And I'm not much into single bars."

Ah, the never ending single-girl question of where to meet men? Dani might not be on the active market for a man, but she knew how hard the shopping for a guy could be.

Hey, that was more great fodder for a routine.

She leaned down and jotted a note to herself.

Allie eyed the notebook. It was a funny look. Not a funny-ha-ha look, but a nervous sort of look.

As a matter of fact, now that Dani thought

about it, a number of employees had eyed her
orange notebook with that same weird intensity.
As if it were somewhat dangerous.

"Is there a problem, Allie?"

"Uh, no." Allie sounded hesitant.

"If something's wrong, I do hope you'll feel
free to talk to me about it. I meant what I said
about having an open door policy."

Allie offered her a weak smile. "Sure," she
said, and turned to leave.

Suddenly Dani had an idea.

"Hey, Allie, about how to meet men . . . I
might have a suggestion for you."

Allie turned back around. "A suggestion?"

"Well, it's sort of outside-the-box. But that's
just the kind of thinking I'm hoping we can
inspire here at Hamlin. But this isn't about
Hamlin, it's about you and meeting men. I have a
brother. Do you have any?"

"Three," Allie said with a sisterly-sigh that
Dani recognized.

"Three? Wow. One's more than I can handle.
But then you'll understand when I say I'm dating someone, and my big brother isn't dealing
with it well. He's set me up with drinks with
someone from his office. I said yes, just to get
him off my back, but really I'm not on the market. That's what's great about tonight's date . . .
it isn't serious."

Her comic date wasn't serious. Dani smiled. There was a bit there. Dating a comic. Okay, so Luke wasn't a comic, but he owned a comedy club.

Still, with some embellishment it could be part of a routine . . .

She jotted dating comics in her book.

Allie watched her.

"Sorry," Dani said. "Where was I?"

"You're not serious about the man you're dating."

"Ah, right. Since I'm already casually dating someone, and since you said that meeting a nice guy is hard, I had an idea. There are many things in the world that are questionable, but my brother—despite the fact he's pigheaded and overbearing—is a reliable judge of character. He's arranged for me to have drinks with a guy he works with on Friday. If he set me up with a guy, the guy must be pretty stellar."

She paused, then added, "This has absolutely nothing to do with work. Feel free to tell me no. But my idea is maybe, if you wanted to meet someone, you might be interested in going in my place to meet with this Sam."

"But he'll be expecting you," Allie said.

"Which is why you'll show up and tell him I had some emergency meeting. An emergency textbook meeting." They both smiled at that. "If you like him, you could buy him a drink on me. If not, you'd just leave and we're both off the hook."

"When is this?"

"Friday."

"Well," Allie said slowly. "I had this date with a half gallon of rocky road ice cream, but I suppose that could wait."

"Great. You're really helping me out."

"It's my pleasure," Allie said. She glanced at the notebook, then said, "Well, I'd better be going."

"Have a nice night, and thanks again. I'll give you the details Friday."

Allie left, shutting the door behind her.

Dani strummed her fingers on the notebook and watched her assistant leave the office.

What was up? Allie seemed more at ease around her, but there was still an undercurrent of tension. And the rest of the office was worse. They still seemed to be on pins and needles whenever she was around.

Dani just didn't understand it. She'd done everything she could to be friendly, to try and demonstrate that she wanted an open-door policy for the staff.

And yet they seemed to be getting more nervous around her, rather than less.

She needed to figure out why.

Dani glanced at her watch.

She didn't have time to puzzle it out tonight. She had a date.

Her heart raced at the thought.

A date without Mart's interruption.

She was smiling as she left the office.

It was going to be a good night.

From the Comedy Journals of Dani Sinclair:

Remember the old adage about two's a company and three's a crowd? There was never a place it was more true than on a date . . .

Chapter Four
Meet the Parents

There are some truths in life that are indisputable and undeniable. The first of those truths on any single-woman's-life-truths list was first dates suck.

But as Dani hurried home from the office and got ready for her date with Luke, she figured that they'd already been through an awful first date when she went to his club, so there was room for optimism.

Granted, most of that first date she'd spent by herself at the table waiting for him and watching the comics. And before Luke rejoin her and they could really get the date going her brother had showed up and dragged her away.

But still, she was counting it as a first date, which meant tonight was a second date and could be perfect.

Promptly at six-thirty, the doorbell rang.

Perfect. Tonight was going to go in the record books as a most perfect date.

She opened the door and right on cue, Luke whistled appreciatively. "You look wonderful."

"Thank you. Come on in while I get my wrap." May evenings could still be cool in Western Pennsylvania.

As she let him in she realized just how bad her apartment looked, but she was determined not to let embarrassment mar the date. "I still haven't had a chance to unpack everything, so just excuse my mess."

"How long have you been here?"

"Just a week in the apartment. I was staying at a hotel on I-90 while I waited for the movers to arrive with my stuff. And with work, I haven't had time to do more than dig for the essentials."

Luke stood in the midst of her chaotic living room waiting for her to get her wrap. Boxes lined the walls, leaving labyrinth-like paths.

She came through one of the openings, a gold wrap covering her simple black dress.

This was going to be a fantastic evening.

He'd been thinking about it—fantasizing even—all day.

"I've got a special night planned for our first date. First—" He stopped abruptly when he noticed Dani's smile had abruptly faded. "Is there a problem?"

As a matter of fact, she was actually frowning.

"You jinxed it," she accused.

"Pardon?" he asked, absolutely lost.

Women were a mystery, for the most part, but having worked with comics, whose minds also worked in an entirely foreign way from the rest of human-kind, Luke felt he was pretty good at keeping up with abrupt twists and turns.

At least, as good as any man could be.

But at the moment, looking at Dani's upset expression, he felt lost.

"I was counting my visit to your club as our first date."

"We spent less than fifteen minutes together. You can't count that. If we count that, then we're in for it because it was horrendous, between me being on the phone and your brother showing up."

"All first dates are horrible. It's just the nature of the beast. So if you had counted Friday as our horrible, terrible first date, then this would be our second date. And everyone knows that second dates have so much more potential for greatness. But you jinxed us and now we're doomed. We probably won't see it coming. Like some jet falling out of the sky, it's waiting. Waiting to fall on us and crush any hopes of a fantastic night."

He laughed, sure she was teasing, but when she didn't join him, he sobered. "You're serious?"

"As a heart attack. Luke, I've been on many, many first dates—well, not *many* as in I'm loose, but enough to have long since proved the postulate that all first dates are always awful is truth. You never go on a second date hoping for a repeat performance, you go praying that the stars will shift back into their normal alignments in the heavens and that the universe will right itself. You get to enjoy yourself and not worry about what horror is waiting for you just around the corner."

Luke laughed. "You're crazy."

She grabbed the glorified scarf thing she'd retrieved and threw it over her shoulders.

They started walking toward his car, Dani didn't pause their first-date discussion.

". . . Take my seventh grade first first date. He took me bowling. I beat him . . . and dropped the bowling ball on his foot, breaking it. The cast kept him from playing in our school's regional basketball playoffs. He was our start point guard.

We lost. No one in my school ever really forgave me for that one. All through high school an occasional joke about broken feet and bowling balls was bandied about. That was my first inkling that first dates suck."

"They couldn't have all been that bad." He opened her door, then walked around to his own side of the car. He got in and she kept going.

". . . food poisoning, poison ivy and a lacerated scalp led three of my first dates to end in emergency rooms."

"They weren't your fault."

"Actually, the head lac was because we were walking in the woods and I leaned against a dead sapling that severed about six feet up and landed on his head. The poison ivy was my fault because I decided a picnic might be a safe date."

"The food poisoning?"

"I picked the restaurant."

"But—"

He was torn between sympathy and laughter. He tried for the first, but did allow a small chuckle to sneak out. If she noticed, she didn't take offense.

He turned onto State Street.

"And then, there was my first high school date. My brother *just happened* to show up at the same movie, and sat right behind us."

"That's not so bad."

"You don't know my brother." She paused.

"Actually, you do. Tall guy, ruined what we're obviously not going to count as our first date, because you jinxed it."

"Well, tonight is our first date, and you haven't chosen the activity or the restaurant, so we're bound to have a wonderful time."

"Maybe we should just go back to my place and watch television. Television should be safe."

"I don't want to belittle your decorating abilities, but Dani, I'm not sure we could find a television at your apartment, much less find someplace to sit and watch it."

She sighed. "You're right."

"Now, we're going out to the lovely restaurant, and we're going to do all the things first date couples do. Get to know each other, laugh at each other's bad jokes."

"Go ahead, be optimistic," she groused. "It won't help, you know. We're doomed."

"See, I've already learned something valuable, you're a pessimist."

"I'm a realist."

"It's going to be just fine, Dani."

"Famous last words."

Dani found herself relaxing, even as she told herself she had to be vigilant. But being on constant guard was hard. Luke was charming and, despite the fact he'd assured her he didn't do stand-up, he was funny.

They made it through the appetizers at Waves, a beautiful restaurant on the bayfront. Unfortunately, the bayfront wasn't that far from her brother's downtown apartment in the old Boston Store. She tried to reassure herself that he wouldn't pose a problem. After all, Mart and Connie had childbirth classes tonight. She'd called Connie at lunch and double checked that they were still going. They were. That should tie up Mart's night and limit his ability to play detective.

"I do think you need to spend more time at the club," he said. "Your first date sagas are a stand-up bit in and of themselves."

"They're not really stand-up, more verbal journals. Verbal memoirs."

He shrugged. "They're unique and funny. They could work on stage."

"I've been thinking about that." He looked blank, and she added, "About your offer."

"Which offer is that?"

"Open Mic Night. I might give it a try. I mean, I think I have some good material. I'm not sure it's really stand-up, and I know it's not a whole act by any stretch of the imagination. But I started out as a drama major in college. Comedy isn't quite what I imagined doing, but it might be fun."

"What made you switch your major from drama?" he asked.

Dani lost track of the conversation as she looked across the restaurant, unable to believe her eyes.

"My parents," she murmured.

"It can be hard to escape parental expectation. But—"

"No, I mean, my parents just walked into the dining room." Dani sunk in her seat, hoping to escape their notice. If she was lucky, they'd walk right by.

Then she remembered that Luke had jinxed them and didn't hold out much hope.

What were her parents doing in Erie anyway?

They were supposed to be in Florida, soaking up those retirement rays. Dani had often thought so many retirees went to Florida in hope that the sun would preserve them, turning them from old grapes into raisins. Dried, but able to maintain a shelf-life a lot longer than a grape.

"To answer your question, yes, they were why I switched to a business degree, but that's neither here nor there. They're here and the first date curse remains unbroken." She paused a moment and added, "Actually, I think we may achieve an all time record for worst first date tonight."

"Come on, it can't be that bad?"

"No, it's worse. You just don't know. Mom might be on my side and try to save us, but my dad? Okay, here's an example. My dad hired my brother to trail me on dates. He makes most over-protective fathers look like slackers. Our only hope is that they don't see me. If it happens, I'll make for the front door, while you pay the bill. We'll rendevous outside, away from dad's prying eyes." The stupid maitre d' was leading her parents right towards them. She scrunched down further into her seat.

Closer.

Closer.

They both had tans and were laughing over something. She knew the minute the smiles froze on their respective faces that the gig was up. There was no escape. No rendevous outside. No end of the first-date curse.

She unhunched herself and sat up, admitting defeat. "They've seen me. It's all over. Brace yourself."

"Danielle," her father called out, right on cue.

Both her parents abandoned the maitre d' and made a beeline to her table.

"Honey," her mother said, her face alight with one of her smiles.

"Mom. Dad." She pasted, what she hoped was a convincing smile on her face. "What are you doing here?"

"We live here in Erie, remember?" Her father said. "So do you now."

"But weren't you supposed to be in Florida for a few more weeks?"

"When the doctor moved up Connie's due date, we decided to move up our departure date. I wouldn't want to miss the birth of my first grandchild." Her mother looked fantastic. A hint of a tan, her hair dyed a subtle dark blond that hid all the grey, and a huge smile on her face.

"And is this Mart's friend Sam that he told us he was fixing you up with?" her father asked. Both her parents were smiling.

"No, this is my friend, Luke. Luke, my parents, Jeff and Dell Sinclair."

"Nice to meet you," they said in polite unison.

"Are you one of Dani's new colleagues?" her mother asked.

"No, just a friend," Luke answered for her.

"Luke's the man Mart told you about. The one that rescued me my first day of work."

"Why don't we join you two and get to know your new friend?" her father asked.

"Jeff, I'm sure they don't want us old folks butting in on their date." She shot Dani a look of apology.

Before Dani could come up with an excuse, Luke said, "Please, we'd be delighted."

Her parents settled in. "So, Mart gave us a brief synopsis, but why don't you give us the whole story of how you met my daughter." There was no question in her father's voice. It was an order, plain and simple.

Dani started, "I don't see how that matters—"

But before she could tell her parents to butt out, Luke said, "Well, Dani had a bit of car trouble, and I went back to offer her a ride, when she hit me with a door."

"You hit him?" her mother asked.

"There were extenuating circumstances. You see, it was a killer-bug and . . ."

"Two hours. My watch says it was just two hours," Dani said again as they were driving back to her place. "Mom was great, but Dad?"

"It wasn't that bad. Your parents were actually very nice."

"But two hours?" Variations of two-hours was all she'd been able to manage the first part of the ride.

Her two-hour mantra was better than Luke's, who hadn't said anything since he'd gotten into the car.

"It did seem a bit longer," he finally admitted.

"Longer?" Dani parroted. "That's not a strong enough word. It seemed like we were stuck in some weird space-time-continuum abnormality. Like a Star Trek, living this day over-and-over loop. *So, Luke, what do you do for a living? You mean you can make money being funny? Oh, you're not funny, you just run the club. A club? Isn't that a fancy way of saying you own a bar?"*

"Hey, don't knock it. That's when your mom reminded your father that *Cheers* was a bar and he'd liked Sam Malone."

"Ah, but that led to a half hour discussion about my years in Los Angeles, hanging out with all those actors."

"Did you ever meet any actors?"

"A few. Well, a few if you count an extra who played an Orc in the *Lord of the Rings*, and another who was a centaur in *Narnia.* My father was sure I was running with druggies and degenerates."

"What did you do in LA?" Luke asked turned off State Street and onto 38th Street.

"Worked as an assistant editor, then editor." She shook her head. "Two hours? It seemed so much longer. And what do you think the odds are that of all the restaurants in Erie, my parents would come into Waves."

"It is a popular spot."

"You and I both know it had nothing to do with it being a popular restaurant. It didn't even have anything to do with the fact my brother doesn't live far from the bay." She waited.

Finally, Luke said the words. "You're right. I jinxed us by calling this our first date."

"I didn't want to say I told you so—"

He laughed. "You don't have to. I'll say it for you. You told me so."

"I don't think I've eaten a meal that fast since, well, I don't know when."

"I appreciated the effort, unfortunately, we had the world's slowest waitress, and the cooks must have gone out and big-game hunted that meat, because I don't think I've ever had a meal take that long to be served. It was all part of the curse I rained down upon us," Luke admitted. "But telling your parents we were meeting a friend for dessert was brilliant, but . . ."

"Yes, but." She shook her head.

Luke pulled up in front of Dani's. "Did he really ask for my social security number?"

"I'm pretty sure he did. Along with your mother's maiden name." She paused. "If I were a comedian, this would make a perfect bit. Double dating with dad. Maybe that will be my first act."

He sounded more serious. "You're still thinking about trying your hand at Open Mic Night?"

Was she?

Part of her—the part who used to love performing in school plays—wanted to. The other part that had spent years working to make a name for herself in the publishing world, knew it would be a waste of time. She had a huge task in front of her, and didn't have time to play on stage.

She just didn't know which part was bigger, so she shrugged.

"You could come down to the club this Thursday night and see how the other amateurs handle things."

"Are you asking me for another date?" Dani might not know if she really wanted to try her hand at stand-up, but she did know she wanted to see Luke again. "Because if you are, we've definitely used up the first-date curse."

"Yes, I was."

She laughed. "I have meetings all day tomorrow. Could we make it next week?"

"Next week then. So will it be our second or third date?" he asked.

"I suggest we stop counting."

"Are there other unlucky numbers?"

"I don't know, but I don't want to tempt fate." She realized they'd been just sitting in the car for a while. "I should go in. I'd invite you in, but I have work tomorrow."

"I understand. Odds are your parents are tailing us anyway. I should have watched our back."

"You could walk me to the door, though. Even

if they are following us, they can't fault you for being a gentleman."

"Sit tight a minute and I'll really impress them." Luke walked around and opened her car door.

The courtesy wasn't necessary, and she knew as an independent, modern career woman, she should protest, but she didn't. It was sweet.

He walked up to the apartment building's door. "Is it permissible to kiss on a second date?"

"No more counting, remember? And yes, I'd say it would be permissible." She stepped closer and couldn't help but notice he smelled good. She wasn't sure how to describe it other than he smelled just like she imagined he would. Warm. Inviting. "A kiss would be welcomed even."

They stood a moment under the golden glow of the door's lamp. Slowly, he moved towards her, his lips gently touching hers in a slow introduction.

It wasn't too hard or too soft. Not too long, but he certainly wasn't rushing it.

As they pulled apart, Dani thought, "That was a perfect first kiss." Actually, it took a moment for her to realize she hadn't just thought the words, she'd said them.

Luke was smiling, looking pleased at the comment. "Ah, so first dates are notoriously bad, but first kisses aren't?"

"Some first kisses are, but not this one." She unlocked the door, then turned. "Good night, Luke."

"Night." He turned and walked back toward his car. She stood a moment, just watching him, then closed the door and walked up to her second floor apartment.

It had been a date to go down in her dating annals as the worst ever. It was nice to see her parents, but not like this.

But she had learned more about Luke that she had with any other first or second dates. He was thirty-two, had never been married and was an only child. He'd been in one other serious relationship, but his ex had left to pursue her own career. In the years since, he'd dated, but nothing serious. He'd been too occupied with Chuckles.

She looked at all the boxes. She'd promised herself she'd unpack at least one a night. But truth be told, she just couldn't find the energy.

She'd rather just head to bed and try and recover.

From the Comedy Journals of Dani Sinclair:

There are certain, undisputable facts. Dryers eat socks. If you're in an accident, you're never wearing your good panties—

they're bound to be in the dryer, with the one sock that wasn't eaten. And a huge, undisputable fact is that families delight in sharing embarrassing stories at the most inopportune moments. But an even bigger truth is that first dates suck, but with the right man, it's possible not to mind too much . . .

Chapter Five
Regifting

"**Y**ou pawned Sam off on your assistant?" was Mart's salutation when Dani made the mistake of answering her phone on Monday morning.

She'd spent the days after her date with Luke concentrating on the mounds of office work. She'd gone through all the personnel files, and had taken meetings with almost everyone who worked at the company, at every level.

She'd decided that though her predecessor had not had wonderful taste in decorating offices, he had managed to compile a great staff. Hamlin might be a small publisher located well outside the New York mainstream, but they'd managed to hire the best in the business.

She'd still been at her desk last Friday, hard at

71

it, when Allie had headed off to meet Dani's blind date, Sam.

Allie had come in this morning, rhapsodizing about him.

Dani tried to sound affronted at this *pawning* comment. "Of course I didn't pawn your friend off. I'm rather hurt you'd even suggest something like that. It's just that we had a bit of a publishing emergency here and I couldn't get away. I didn't want to leave him hanging, and I didn't have a number to call, so I sent someone to let him know."

She could hear his sigh over the phone. "I'd say I'd try again for you and Sam, but all I've been hearing is Allie-this and Allie-that. He's head-over-heels."

Since they were on the phone, Dani didn't even have to try and suppress her smile, but she did try and sound as if she'd regretted the missed opportunity. "Well, that's too bad. But I suppose it's hard to miss what you've never known, so don't worry, I'll get by."

"Oh, I know you will. You still owe me a blind-date and I'm setting one up for this Friday. Drinks. Same time, same place, same scarf."

"Mart, you do remember I'm dating someone, right?"

"Oh, I know all about that. I talked to Mom and Dad. They said he doesn't seem like a serial killer, but you're not married yet, and you're going to love Dan."

"Oh, come on, Mart. Dan and Dani? It could never work between us if only because of the name issue."

"You know Mom's friend Jean and her husband Gene have never seemed to have a problem."

"I—"

"You owe me, so be there."

Fighting with Mart was like beating her head against a brick wall, only worse. "Fine."

As if on cue, Allie walked into the office. "I'm sorry, but your two-thirty is here."

"Sorry, Mart. I've got to go. I have a meeting." Without waiting for his response, she hung up, then told Allie, "Thanks. You saved me from my brother's lecture about regifting his blind date."

Allie hesitated. "I'm sorry he's giving you grief, but thank you. Sam was . . ." She appeared to be searching for words to describe Sam and finally just gave up. She just smiled a ga-ga sort of smile and said, "Well, he's perfect."

"From what my brother said, apparently Sam feels the same about you."

"Really?" Allie's whole face lit up.

Dani nodded. "According to Mart Sam's been all Allie-this and Allie-that all day."

If her assistant smiled any broader, she was going to sprain a cheek muscle. "Thanks, Dani.

And Melissa down in the mailroom said if you ever need to regift another blind date, she's in the market?"

"Really? It just so happens . . ."

From the Comedy Journals of Dani Sinclair:

I once mentioned that I liked frogs to an aunt. Ever since, she's given me frogs whenever a present has been called for. For years I valiantly held onto them, but eventually, my pad wasn't big enough for me and them, so I gave them away.

I regifted them.

Which is what got me to thinking that regifting could work in non-gift situations as well. When someone sets you up on a blind date, or if you go out with a man who seems nice enough, but just doesn't click, why waste him? A nice guy is a treasure. So if one doesn't work for you, pass him onto a friend in need . . .

Chapter Six
Stand Up and Take a Bow

Thursday night, Dani just couldn't stop smiling. Luke looked wonderful and it wasn't a first date . . . well, life was looking good.

"So," he said slowly. "No brothers at the door, and no emergencies at the club. Maybe, just maybe we're in for a quiet, evening?"

"We can hope. It's starting nice."

"So, tell me about work?"

They were sitting at the corner table in Chuckles. It was still early enough that things were quiet. The stage was empty and people were trickling in and filling the surrounding tables.

Dani had looked forward to this dinner all day.

Oh, who was she trying to fool—she'd looked forward to it since leaving him last week.

She had a briefcase filled with papers she needed to go over tonight before bed, and there was still tons of unpacking she should probably do sometime before her first anniversary in the apartment. But that all took a dim second to spending time with Luke.

"Work is progressing, although not as quickly as I'd hoped. So many people in the office are still walking on eggshells around me," she stopped, gave him a stern look and added, "No lame comments again on how painful that must be."

Luke make a scouting sign. "It hadn't even crossed my mind."

She shot him another look and he laughed. "Okay, so maybe it crossed my mind, but it didn't cross my lips. After that first attempt fell flat, I realized it was a dud."

"I guess the highlight of my week was the blind date my brother set me up on. And before you start doubting my attraction for you, let me hasten to add, I regifted him."

"Pardon?"

"Well, good catches are hard to find, and if my brother set me up with him, odds are he was indeed a good catch. Why waste him? I regifted him to my assistant. She was so pleased that she mentioned her friend was actively looking, so when Mart offered—well, offered is generous, he ordered—me to meet another of his friends, I regifted that one as well."

"That's brilliant," Sherri said from behind Dani. "I didn't mean to eavesdrop. I was coming over to see what you wanted to drink and happened to overhear, and like I said, that's brilliant. If your brother has any other friends he'd like to set you up with, I'd be interested in a regifting."

"What nights don't you work?"

"Hey. Ladies. Hello." Luke waved a hand. "There's a man sitting here. And as the only member of my gender present, I feel I must protest on behalf of all of men everywhere. We're not chattel to be bartered off."

"Never said you were," Dani assured him with a smile. "But blind dates are like gifts. You never know what's under the wrapping paper. Some of the prettiest paper covers true duds, and some plain wrapping covers a diamond. My brother would only pick out diamonds for me. So, why waste them? I'm not bartering, not getting anything out of the regifting except a happy sense of helping friends meet nice guys."

"But . . ." Luke started to protest, but he seemed to come up blank for an argument. "Still, I'm not sure it's right."

"Right or wrong, I'm in," Sherri assured them.

She took their drink orders then hurried away with a big smile on her face.

Anxious to avoid a lecture from Luke about bartering men, she tried, "How was your week? I saw Chris the other night. He said hi, and don't forget to get your oil changed soon."

"Don't think I've forgotten the regifting, but I've decided in the interest of avoiding another dating fiasco to let it slide." He took a sip of water. "So, to answer your question, my week was busy. Thanks for passing along Chris's reminder. I was going to call next week and set up a complete once-over. And—"

Dani was interrupted by a tiny blond at the microphone. "Hi, everyone. I'm Cassie from WLVH Radio Station's Night Calls. I left WLVH's Ted and his new wife at the station tonight handling the calls in order to be with you all here. So, I'll be your host for Open Mic Night. We've got a nice list of new talent on our sign up sheet. Let's start with Mike. Mad Mike Martin, come on up."

Cassie left the microphone and a small man with wild black curly hair came out of the audience and took his place center-stage. "Hi, everyone. I'm Mad Mike Martin. Mike here at Open Mic Night. Mike at Open Mic Night. Try saying that one three times fast."

Dani felt bad for him and forced a loud chuckle. She was pretty much the only one.

The small, doughy, dark-haired man smiled in her direction, took a deep breath, and started back into his routine.

It didn't get any better.

"Mike's been a regular since I opened," Luke said. "He kept pestering for a chance to try his hand at stand-up. He's why I decided to put the microphone up for amateur grabs. Some of his jokes have actually gotten better."

If this was better, Dani was glad she missed the worse. Poor Mike finished to lukewarm applause from the audience.

"Thanks, Mike," Cassie said. "Next, we have a virgin comic."

Whistles rang out through the audience. "Dirty, dirty minds," Cassie said with an emphatic tsk which got bigger laughs than any of Mike's jokes. "A virgin performer. She's never been on stage, but Sherri guarantee that her regifting bit will have you all laughing out loud . . ."

Dani scanned the room for Sherri and found her smiling broadly from behind the bar. "You'll rock," she mouthed. At least that's what Dani thought she mouthed. It could just as easily have been, "You'll suck," or "You'll stink."

Maybe she was wrong. Maybe Sherri told another budding comic about the regifting.

"Dani Sinclair."

So much for the first-date jinx being over and

done with. If anything, it had just gotten much worse. She'd talked about trying out, thought about it a lot even, but she'd made no real plans to try.

Dani looked at Luke for support. He didn't look as pleased as Sherri, but all he did was shrug.

"Dani?" Cassie called when no one came up on stage. "Dani, don't get cold feet now."

"Luke, help," she whispered.

Part of Luke wanted to do just that, help her. Get her out of going on stage. Do whatever it took to stop her.

But Luke knew Dani had been thinking about doing just this. And though she had a touch of cold-feet, he knew deep down that she'd love it.

He also knew, although Dani was totally oblivious, that she had a natural sense of comic timing. Dani was a natural. Her normal conversation was peppered with kernels of bits. With a little experience, she could be good. He'd been surrounded by comics long enough to know that.

But he'd been surrounded by comics long enough to know he didn't want to date one.

"Luke?" she repeated.

Maybe she'd hate it.

This one small taste might convince her that the world of publishing was so much preferable to that of comedy.

Either way, he couldn't let her hide behind him. One day she might resent it. He forced a smile and said, "Go on, give it a shot. The room's still fairly empty, so who'll know?"

"You. You'll see me up there and realize what a big doofus I really am."

"I asked you out after our great bug-gut introduction. Do you really think a bit of stand-up could scare me away? I mean, I started dating you knowing you were a very funny lady."

"Funny, weird? Or funny, ha-ha?"

"Dani Sinclair, Sherri's pointed you out." A spotlight hit her. "Might as well just give in and come up," Cassie said. "Come on, ladies and gentlemen, let's try to coax our newest reluctant comic up on stage."

Cassie started clapping and the rest of the sparse audience joined in. Dani faced the inevitable and stood up.

"Ah, there she is," Cassie cried. "Dani, everyone."

The audience continued clapping as she took center stage. Luke could see she was nervous, but despite that, she looked at home up there as she adjusted the microphone.

"Hi, everyone. I'm Dani and I'm going to confess, I hadn't planned on coming up here tonight. But since I'm here, I'd like to address the ladies in the audience. Ladies, have you ever been set up by a friend, or family member? Someone whose judgement you trust? If the man doesn't work out, or if you already have a great guy and aren't interested, why waste a potential nice-guy by just throwing him back? I say, regift him . . ."

Luke watched Dani intently. She didn't behave like a stand-up virgin. She had an impeccable sense of timing, and she wisely wasn't trying to do jokes, but rather was doing a running commentary on regifting dates. Then she segued into a bit on first-dates.

Though she didn't mention him by name, she did talk about a date that was certainly their date. The knot that had formed in the pit of Luke's stomach when Cassie had called Dani onto the stage, tightened and twisted. She was using him as fodder. He hated it. It reminded him of—

"She's good, isn't she?" Sherri said from behind him.

Luke didn't bother to answer. He watched as Dani left the stage to the sound of genuine applause and made her way back to him.

Her expression was one of dazed excitement. "That was fun. Well, fun in an I-might-puke-at-any-second sort of way. I can't remember the last time I felt so invigorated. It's—" she broke off, leaned over the table and kissed him. "Thank you."

"It wasn't me, it was Sherri."

It was as if she'd just noticed Sherri. "Thanks, Sherri. I would have probably spent the next few years hemming and hawing over whether or not I should try it. You gave me the nudge—well, not exactly nudge, it was more of a big push—I needed."

"I think I followed most of that," Sherri said, smiling almost as broadly as Dani. "And what I gather is you're not mad, that you're apprecia- tive. So, you're welcome. I'll just let the two of you get back to your date."

Dani sat back in her seat, still wearing her ga- ga over life sort of look. "Amazing. That was simply amazing."

"Glad you enjoyed it. Everyone should try something like that at least once." Once. It would be great if once was enough for Dani, but from her happy expression, he had his doubts.

As if she'd read his thoughts, she said, "Yeah, but sometimes once isn't enough."

"Is this one of those times?"

"I think it might be."

That knot in Luke's stomach twisted so hard it turned into a lead ball, weighing him down.

He listened to Dani rhapsodize about the expe- rience trying to maintain some semblance of enthusiasm for her benefit.

Maybe she noticed he was quiet, but he doubt- ed it. She was still flying high. Her words finally stopped tumbling so fast as they ate and listened to the rest of the amateur acts, but her excitement was still evident. He got up a few times, but managed to spend most of the evening at Dani's table.

Finally, around ten she glanced at her watch. "I really should go. This was wonderful."

"It was nice." He stood and walked her toward the back door of the club.

"Would you mind if I came back next Thursday?" she asked. "Unless . . ." she let the one word hang there.

Luke knew it had hung there a bit too long. He smiled. "Yes, that would be great. But I'd like to see you sooner, if you have time earlier in the week?"

"Maybe Monday?"

He smiled. "Monday. I'll call the office and we'll decide what we'll do."

"Great." She stood on tip-toe and kissed him. "Goodnight, Luke."

Luke watched her leave, then walked back to the bar and went behind it. "I'll take over here. Why don't you take another round of drink orders."

"Luke," Sherri said. "I didn't mean to cause problems."

"I'm fine." He knew he'd sounded more than a little snappish, so he added, "Really, it's fine."

"I didn't think about, well, you know. I just

didn't think when I told Cassie to call her up first."

"No problem. She wanted to do it." He wiped down the bar, though it was pristine. He needed something to do.

"She's not Caitlyn," Sherri said softly.

"I know that."

"Maybe you do know it, but when you saw her go up on stage, you forgot. But she's not Caitlyn. Dani's not a comic. She's a woman who runs a publishing house that publishes college text books—a woman who happens to be funny and have a great sense of time. She's simply flirted with the idea of comedy."

"But she was good." He wished she hadn't been. He wished he'd been wrong and she'd tanked. And because that's what he wished, he felt like a first class heel.

"Yes, she was good. I'd heard enough to know she wasn't going to flop, but she was better than I could have imagined."

"She started out a drama major in college. She likes being center stage."

"I saw you watching her. There's something there. I've also watched you since Caitlyn. Don't do it Luke, don't push her away like the other ones. She's not Caitlyn."

"I'll remember," he promised Sherri. It should be an easy promise to keep because anyone meeting Dani would know that her comic ability was the only trait Dani shared with his ex.

It should be easy, so he wasn't sure why it wasn't.

From the Comedy Journals of Dani Sinclair:

I don't have any observations or ideas to put in this journal tonight. I'm still flying too high from my few minutes on the stage. I've missed that kind of feeling. The last time I felt this was playing Amneris in Aida at the Playhouse. Strutting across the stage, singing Elton John's songs, knowing everyone was watching me. That's why I wanted to major in drama. I loved that rush. But tonight was better. They weren't watching a character, they were watching me.

It might not be very CEOish, might not be the wisest course for someone so new to this position, but I can't wait to try it again.

Chapter Seven
Expiration Dates

Two weeks.

Dani sat at her desk on the Thursday two weeks after her first time at the microphone and smiled. Two weeks of seeing Luke as often as possible. Things were going so well between them.

Oh, they were both busy, and worked very different hours, so seeing each other could take juggling, but it was worth it.

Luke was—

She cut herself off. She'd been down this road too many times recently. It was easy to slip into a Luke-fest, itemizing his many wonderful qualities. There were just so many. He was funny, sweet, and—

She cut herself off.

Enough.

She had two more hours of work to do, then she was leaving for the club and her third time on stage.

She glanced at the orange notebook. It went everywhere with her lately. It had become a cross between a journal and a comedy workbook. She knew she needed work on stage. Frequently, rather than doing a true bit, her time in front of the microphone was more a journalesque monologue.

She itched to go over tonight's act, but she was stern with herself.

She had work. Hamlin was her job and it had to be her priority. She'd worked so hard for this chance and she wasn't going to blow it because she had a bit of a stand-up bug. This was the perfect place. She was home in Erie, and had a challenging job to do. Add to that, she'd found a wonderful guy, and a fun new avocation. Okay, no more thoughts about Luke or the club.

She realized despite lecturing herself, she was holding the notebook.

"Ms. Sinclair?"

"Joan. What can I do for you?"

Joan was an editorial assistant, and from what Dani could tell, she was excellent at her job.

"I was told you needed these figures?"

Joan's eyes were darting nervously from Dani to anywhere but Dani. She shifted from one foot to the other, then made a split-second eye contact with Dani, before looking away again.

Dani couldn't tell just what Joan was looking at, but it was obvious from her fidgeting that she was nervous.

She tried to think of something, anything to say to put the woman at ease. "Thanks for bringing the figures in."

"You're welcome." Joan's eyes still darted about. Back and forth, back and forth.

She decided to cut right to the chase. "Joan, is something wrong?"

"No, Ms. Sinclair."

"Dani, remember? And are you sure there's nothing wrong? Nothing you want to talk to me about? I'm always willing to listen."

"No, but thank you. Everything's fine." And so saying, the woman hurried out of the office, whacking her leg on a bookshelf as she left. It barely slowed down her hasty retreat. She limped out of the office.

Weird.

It was just weird.

Dani had done everything she could to show she had an open door at work, that she was willing to listen, more than that, that she encouraged dialogue. Nothing she said or did seemed to help.

She was at her wit's end. People tripped, fell, banged and in general, looked nervous whenever she was in the vicinity.

The first days she'd been so busy trying to acclimate, that she'd just chalked up their nervousness as newness.

But last week—though she was still busy—she had slowed down enough to notice the odd state of her relations with the staff, and she'd worked at setting people at ease.

All for nothing. They were still as freaked out as ever.

She wished she knew what to do. She didn't think she was one of those scary bosses. She'd had a number of those herself, and she just couldn't seem to fit herself into that profile. She never yelled, she'd tried to be reasonable in her expectations.

Scary bosses.

Ogres.

Memories of bosses she'd loved, and those she hadn't came flooding back.

She opened her notebook and started to scribble.

Dani wasn't sure she was feeling better by the time she got to the club. Normally, sketching ideas was a great way to relax. But this time, she was still perplexed about the situation at work. Maybe Luke would have an idea.

That was new . . . having someone to share her concerns with. Oh, her parents would listen, but it wasn't the same. Luke had such an easygoing attitude. And he ran a business. A very different business than hers, but he knew what it meant to be in charge, to feel the weight of every decision.

She parked in one of the reserved spaces that Luke had told her to use, and came in the back entrance.

"Hi, Dani," Jon, the bouncer slash everything-man called.

"Hi," she called.

She found Sherri at the bar. "Hey, you're about to be regifted. I've set up two women at work, and both are still dating the guys. I know you're busy here on the weekends, so I set up 'my' blind date for Monday next week, if that works for you."

Sherri was grinning ear-to-ear. "Oh yeah, I can make that work. So, what do we know about him."

Dani pulled up a barstool. "Henry Liniard. He's in banking. Mart's worked with him in the past. Single, never married, big family, but they're out of state. Nice looking, but not GQ. And I have to tell you, making my brother assess the looks of the men he's setting me up with is beyond fun."

Sherri laughed.

"So, how would you rank his butt? Because, you know for me, it's all about the booty, I asked Mart. He turned seven shades of red on that one."

Sherri leaned on the bar and asked dreamily, "How did he describe it?"

"A ten. Firm, high, and not too big. At least that's what I took away from his numerous false starts, stutters and stammers." She handed her a card and the red scarf. "Here's the info."

Sherri stood back up, laughing. "You're really quite wicked, you know."

"Yes, I've been informed . . . by my brother. Often." She glanced around. "Where's Luke?"

"He said you're to meet him in his office."

She slid back the barstool and stood. "Great. See you in a bit."

"If you're cued and not out, I'll come get you. But don't worry about me barging in. I'll knock so you have all kinds of leeway."

Dani was still chuckling as she made her way to Luke's private office, just behind the bar. He'd left the door open, and was standing with his back towards it leafing through a folder as she entered.

She stood a moment, just watching him. She'd missed him. It had only been a full twenty-four hours since they'd grabbed a quick dinner together, and yet it felt longer.

She'd dated in the past, but she'd never counted minutes like she did with Luke. She'd always been self-sufficient, comfortable on her own. She'd enjoy her time together with the men she'd dated, but never minded her time alone.

That was what was different with Luke. She counted those minutes without him, saved funny tidbits to share. She walked up behind him, slipped her arms around his waist and drank in the feel of him.

"Oh, Denesha, you'd better go before my girlfriend catches you." He twirled and pulled her into his arms. "Oh, it's you," he said with a wicked little laugh.

"So, I'm your girlfriend, huh?"

"You don't want to know who Denesha was?"

She laughed. "No. You're so busy that I know you don't have time for anyone but me. But you never answered my question . . . I'm your girlfriend?"

"Are you?"

She kissed him long and hard. "Yeah, I guess I am."

"Well, that's settled. I feel as if I should have a class ring or something to give you to seal the deal."

"Another kiss like that would work just as well." She was pleased he so readily obliged.

"Did you want to get something to eat?"

"I'd rather just spend some time with you until you're called away."

"I'm happy to oblige."

They sat on his rather dilapidated couch, close enough to touch, and simply shared their day. The bits of this and that she'd so carefully stored away, and hoarded for this moment.

Spilling her concerns over work was a relief. ". . . and it's been weeks and things still aren't as easy as I'd like. I walk into a room and conversations cease. Darty eyes, nervous fidgeting. And the accidents. Just about every piece of furniture in the place has been tripped on, or bumped into by one person or another. Why just the other day . . ." She launched into a detailed description of lunchroom nervousness that resulted in a cola-mishap.

Luke laughed at all the right places and then proceeded to assure her that things would settle down. "It might have been weeks, but you're still new. They're still weighing and measuring you. Still probably nervous that you're going to fire them, or make other huge sweeping changes."

"But I'm not. It's a good crew. Most of the changes are more a technique than a personnel thing. Why I—"

There was a knock at the door, then Sherri's muffled voice. "Dani, you're on in two."

Luke practically sprang off the couch, putting distance between them. "You'd better go."

He felt further away than the few feet that separated them.

"Luke, is something wrong?"

"No, of course not. But you're on. You'd better go."

"I—"

"Listen, Dani, stand-up might be some new game for you, but it's my business. If you're getting tired of it, say so now. Don't waste my time, and don't cast my club in a bad light by treating this like some big game."

"I—"

Sherri knocked again. "Dani?"

Luke just cocked his head, and stared at her.

She stood, staring at him a moment, trying to figure out what was wrong. His expression gave nothing away. "I guess I'd better go then."

"I guess you'd better."

"Dinner after?"

"I don't know. I have a lot of work to do."

Dani was confused as she left the office and headed to the stage just as Judy, another of the WLVH DJ's who'd been playing host to the Thursday night open mics, said, ". . . a new club favorite, Dani."

She pasted a smile on her face, trying to mask her agitation, and walked center stage in front of the microphone. She was too flustered to remember any particular bit, so instead, she simply gave a recap of her day.

"Today at work . . ."

Despite her worry about Luke, she fell into the rhythm of her story, reached out and felt the moment she clicked with audience. She was learning to look for that moment. It was a tangible zing that told her she had the audience, that she owned them.

That feeling, that the audience was hers, was such a powerful rush. She might be confused about so many things in her life, but this she owned.

She started talking about work, about employee mishaps, about killer-bugs and bathroom stalls. She rode the rhythm of story and punchline to an exhilarating high. Her only worries about work were how to make it comic, and worries about men and family faded as well.

Dani had enjoyed her other forays into the spotlight, but tonight, was more. She'd found 'it,' found the magic of a perfect set.

She left center stage to the sound of applause and, as if by some magic radar, her line of sight zeroed in on Luke, standing in a corner by the bar.

She was practically jumping with excitement by the time she reached him. "Did you see that? I had them, Luke. I mean, I really had them. I got up there, and forgot the bit I was going to do, so I just talked to them and it worked. I've had moments before, but tonight, it was the whole time. I started in and I just knew that the audience was mine. They laughed and . . ."

She'd run out of words to describe it. So she simply hugged Luke and then kissed his cheek.

It took a moment for her to realize that he wasn't exactly hugging her back, and another moment to realize he was actually just standing stone-still.

For a moment, riding the high of a great set, she'd forgotten their earlier distance. It came flooding back to her completely. She stood back, putting a physical distance between them as well, then let her hands drop to her side. "Luke?"

"Dani, I—"

Her cell phone buzzed in her pocket. She pulled it out to turn it off, and saw that it was a text message. BRUTUS COMING. MEET AT HOSP.

"Luke, whatever this is between us tonight, we do need to talk about it. I want to talk about it. I think we've got something special growing, but there's obviously some things that still need to be worked out. But as much as I want to figure this out, right now I've got to run. I'm about to be an aunt."

His stand-offishness faded instantly. "Do you need a ride?"

"No. I've got it. They're at Hamot, so it's a straight shot from here."

"Okay." He leaned down and kissed her cheek. "I know it's cliché, but this, well tonight wasn't about you, it's me. I have to work it out."

"I'd like to work it out with you. Soon. But right now . . ."

"You've got to run. Go."

She hurried back into the office and grabbed her jacket and purse.

She liked Luke. Liked him more than any man in recent memory. She worried that somehow, they'd blown the tentative relationship. No, not they. Not matter what he said, she worried that *she'd* blown it.

Maybe their dating relationship had gone as far as it could go.

Maybe some relationships just had a time-limit. At least hers had seemed to in the past.

She'd thought what she had with Luke was different, but maybe there was just something about her that only let a relationship go so far.

Dani didn't know, but she pushed her worries to the side. She was about to become an aunt.

From the Comedy Journals of Dani Sinclair:

Maybe there's a time limit on some dating relationships. Like milk in your fridge, they come with definite 'use by dates.' Those types of dates are Expiration Dates, if you will. A casual, dating relationship that seems to go fine, but after a short amount of time that is easily equivalent to the shelf life of milk, they inexplicably go sour. You can't really define one particular moment, you can't pinpoint anything specific that's wrong, but that tentative dating relationship needs to be tossed out. Oh, you can let it hang out in the refrigerator for a few more weeks, but all it will do then is move from soured to curdled, and there's nothing worse than a curdled date.

Chapter Eight
Birds Do It, Bees Do It

It turned out that Mart and Connie were a bit overly optimistic with their baby SOS. They'd felt the baby's arrival was imminent.

It turned out that first babies take a while.

Sometimes a long while.

A very long while.

Which meant Mart had plenty of time to list his grievances against her to their father, while her mom tried to run interference, and Connie, lay ensconced in her birthing bed, panting her way through contractions.

". . . and she skipped out on another date with one of my friends," Mart the tattletale-extraordinaire said. "This time she sent someone named Michelle, and that's all Dan can talk about. He thanked me for arranging it and says he's off the market, which means he's not interested in another blind date with Dani."

"I told you, Dan and Dani. It would have been problematic. Michelle and Dan, no problems there."

"Yes," her mom agreed. "Not a good name combo."

Her father, taking Mart's side, said, "But you know Gene and Jean. They've never had a problem."

"They're special." Dani tried to be calm, after all, the midwife's mantra was birth-should-be-a-serene-experience. "Listen, all of you, I'm an adult. I've managed my own dates for years."

"You still seeing that comic?" Mart asked.

"Club owner. They won't let him near a microphone." She smiled as memories assaulted her. "And yes, I'm still seeing him. But it's casual. I agreed to meet another of your friends, remember?"

After the weirdness tonight, it might not even be casual. Was she still seeing Luke?

He'd been nice enough when she left, offering to give her a ride to the hospital even. And things had seemed fine when she first got there. But then he got distant, and she wasn't sure why.

"We're both busy people, so it can be tricky," she added for good measure. "We're just keeping it casual. That's all I have time for."

"If it was the real deal, you'd both find time, no matter how busy you are." Her father shot her a look that said I'm-the-dad-and-know-what-I'm-talking-about with a bit of you're-an-exasperating-daughter-who's-never-taken-advantage-of-all-my-wisdom mixed in.

"Jeff." There was warning in her mom's voice.

Connie stepped in as well. "Dani-pant has-pant proven-pant she's-pant capable-pant of-pant handling-pant herself-pant." The contraction must have ebbed because she finished in a pant-free rush, "She's not only excelled at everything she's ever tried, from school to her job, but she's managed her life on her own for years. When the time's right, when the man's right, she'll go after it with that kind of vigor and I'm sure she'll succeed. In the meantime . . ."

Connie's expression grew more serious and she took a long breath. "I-pant suggest-pant we-pant leave-pant her-pant be-pant."

"I second that motion," Dani said hurriedly, "and add that maybe rather than worrying about my love-life we concentrate on why we're here. A new baby."

Know your audience . . . any performer knew that. And knowing this audience, Dani added,

"Mom, you're about to become a grandmother. Did you finish that blanket you were knitting?"

Her mother winked, acknowledging she could ride to the rescue. She didn't even need to put on an act to get that grandma-ga-ga look on her face, but before she could launch into her ode to grandmotherhood, Mart interrupted. "Fine. I'll drop it for now, but you'd better show up at that date next week."

Then Mart, who didn't have nearly as many ominous looks as their mother did, could manage a good I'm-the-big-brother-and-know-what's-best look when the occasion called for it. And given the practiced ease he used with it tonight, he felt the occasion did indeed call for it. And must have been practicing, because it was a good superior look.

"Great," Dani replied, careful not to promise anything. The next blind-date was already regifted to Sherri on Monday night.

"So, Mom, about this grandma thing—"

This time it wasn't Mart who interrupted her mother, it was Connie.

"I think maybe," she started, then a wave of concentration swept over her face, "you'd-pant best-pant call-pant the-pant midwife-pant."

"Maybe I should go?" Dani asked, hopefully.

"Us, too," her father, looking very pale, chimed in. He was on his feet, taking her mom's hand and dragging her out the door before Dani had even collected her purse.

Connie took a deep, cleansing breath. "Dani, I'd like you to stay, if you don't mind. Mart could use the backup."

"Hey, I took all the classes you did," he said.

"Well, then—"

Dani saw her way out and grabbed it. "Well, then I'll be with Mom and Dad." She turned again, ready to flee.

"But," Mart said, stopping her before she got the birthing room door open. "I guess having someone else wouldn't be a bad idea."

There was no way out.

Resigning herself to witnessing the *miracle* of birth, Dani put her stuff back in the corner and stood next to Connie, opposite Mart.

The midwife, a big, redheaded woman with the ability to shout orders like a drill Sergeant, came in, took a look under the sheet and announced, "Looks like we're going to have a baby soon."

From the Comedy Journals of Dani Sinclair:

I don't know why they call unmedicated childbirth natural. It sounds warm and fuzzy. Natural childbirth. In reality, it is warm, if the amount of sweating that goes on is any indication, and my sister-in-law assures me that the details are fuzzy when it's over. She claims all she remembers is them handing her the baby.

As someone who witnessed the birth firsthand, I could fill her in, because I remember a lot more than she does. As a matter of fact, I recall enough to have totally rethought my position on becoming a mother. Of course, becoming a mother is rather a moot point . . . I'd need a significant other first and I don't seem close to finding one of those. Because as much as I can't figure out why anyone would choose to forgo all the good drugs they have to alleviate the pain of childbirth, I have even less of a chance to understand how a male mind works.

Chapter Nine
Life's a Beach

Luke had left a few messages over the week-end, but he hadn't been able to connect with Dani in person. So, on Monday, when he didn't hear *Thanks for calling, but I'm not in right now. Please leave a message at the tone and I'll get back to you as soon as possible*, and instead heard, "Hello?" he felt as if he'd been thrown a curve and sat silent for a moment.

He'd had his message worked out in his head, but hadn't thought of a single thing to say in person.

"Hello?" Dani repeated.

"Dani, uh, it's Luke. Can we see each other outside the club sometime this week? Maybe tomorrow, Tuesday?" he all but blurted out.

Okay, not an *all-but-blurted* at all. He definitely blurted. Brusk and to the point. And he wasn't the least bit sure why he'd felt the need to clarify tomorrow was Tuesday. Dani had a calendar. She had to be aware of the days of the week.

"Luke, I know you left two messages this weekend. I didn't call back right away, because I know weekends are busy, but I'd planned to call you back today."

She paused, then added softly, "I'll confess, I was surprised. I got the impression that things weren't working out. That whatever it was we'd had . . ." He couldn't help but note she didn't name what she thought they had, or rather what *she* had thought they had had. "Well, whatever it was had fizzled and burned itself out."

"I don't think we've fizzled." He probably should say more, try to explain why he'd behaved badly. He should tell her that any distance she'd perceived, any fizzle, was his fault. But he didn't say any of it.

She waited for a moment, maybe hoping he would offer up some reason, but when he couldn't find the words.

Dani finally just said, "Oh."

Anxious to get beyond talk of fizzle and put their dating relationship back on a sizzle sort of track, he said, "I'd very much like to see you somewhere that's not here."

Again, she didn't respond immediately, as if she were waiting for more.

Women.

Talk, talk, talk.

Men realized it was more about actions than words.

Okay, so maybe his actions the other night hadn't said much of anything either.

Knowing he wasn't going to escape an apology, he added, "I'm sorry about the other night. I was in a funk, but that's no excuse. I wanted to kick myself after you left. I really want a chance to redeem myself. Let me make it up to you. A night out, away from the club. Just the two of us."

This time she didn't hesitate. "Yes. I'd like that."

"Tomorrow, then? I'll pick you up at your place at six?"

She agreed, though he sensed a distance there. He was going to have to find some way to overcome that hurdle.

They finished the conversation in short order and Luke breathed out a huge sigh of relief when he finally hung up the receiver. Then he realized he'd forgotten to ask about her brother's new baby.

He jumped as he heard the sound of someone clapping.

Sherri was standing in his office doorway grinning and she clapped. "Good for you. If you let her slip away, I'd have never let you live it down."

He wouldn't have needed Sherri to remind him, he had a feeling a woman like Dani wouldn't be replaced very easily. She was the perfect combination of intelligence and humor. And there was an amazing chemistry between them. Something he'd never experienced before.

It was just seeing her on stage brought back memories. And unfortunately, they weren't good ones. Seeing other comics center-stage didn't give him any problem. Which was a good thing given having a comic in the spotlight was his bread and butter. But someone he was dating, someone he was coming to care about up on stage?

As if she read her mind, Sherri started to remind him for the umpteenth time, "She's not—"

He stopped her. "I know. Really, I do know. And before you feel the need to spell it out for me, I also know that Dani's special. Now that we've cleared all that up, the question is, where am I going to take her?"

Sherri came all the way into the office and took a seat. "Waves?"

Luke shook his head. "Been there, done that and it wasn't what I'd call an unqualified success. Unless you count dining with her parents—

parents who didn't seem overly enthused by me—a success?"

"I don't. But I do count it as a fancy date. The two of you have spent a lot of your time together here, which counts as casual at best. Something not here, not as fancy that's definitely romantic?"

Sherri mused a moment, then looked up and smiled. "As long as you're getting out of here, and don't want to go to a fancy restaurant, why not take it in an entirely different direction? She's been out of town for a long time, and so busy since she arrived, that other than the inside of the club and her office, I bet she hasn't enjoyed many of Erie's attractions. What if you used the date to reintroduce her to what the city has to offer? And while you're reminding her about the city, maybe you'll remind her what a great guy you can be."

"I'm a great guy, Sherri?"

"Maybe."

"Isn't tonight your big night?"

"Yes, but don't change the subject. We're talking about you and Dani. Maybe you've reached a point in the relationship where you both talk about your pasts. It's hard to understand where someone is, if you can't see where they've been."

"I don't want to talk about where I've been. I'd

rather concentrate on where I'm going with Dani."

Sherri shrugged. "Suit yourself. But I think you're wrong."

Wrong or right, Luke didn't want to think about his past. All he wanted to think about was Dani and where this relationship might be leading.

"This is perfect," Dani said, the next night at seven.

They were sitting at a picnic table, along the tree-line next to the water at Lake Erie the next night.

It was still springtime, which meant it was brisk along the lakeshore with the cooler Canadian air blowing in off the water. But that meant this section of the lakeshore was practically deserted.

Dani had forgotten about this aspect of moving home. "I love sunsets here. I spent time in California and saw my share of sunsets on the ocean, but they don't hold a candle to Erie's. Not that I'm biased or anything."

Luke laughed. "I didn't grow up here, but I've learned to appreciate the lake. This time of day especially." He paused, then murmured, "Beautiful."

Dani turned toward him and realized he wasn't

looking at the lake, but at her. She could feel her cheeks warm.

He brushed a piece of her hair back off her face and she felt unsure.

They hadn't talked about what had happened the other night, and Dani didn't want to bring it up. As much as she wanted to understand, she didn't want to ask him what that had been about.

She'd tried to convince herself that Luke had just been out of sorts. Everyone had a bad day now and then, didn't they? She worked at convincing herself that whatever had happened was a fluke.

But as many times as she told herself that, she still couldn't make herself quite believe that's all it was. When she'd come off the stage, riding high from a successful set, he'd pulled back. She wanted to ask him why, to get to the bottom of it, but she didn't want to ruin the evening. He seemed over it, whatever it was.

Maybe it was just a bad day, she told herself for the hundredth time.

So, rather than mention it, rather than question the distance that had suddenly appeared, she said, "Tell me about your family."

"I grew up here in Columbus. Dad was a cop, Mom a teacher. They're in Arizona for a month, visiting my little brother. He's married and has a one-year-old daughter."

"So, you're an uncle. My brother—I know you remember him . . ."

He smiled, just as she intended.

"I meant to ask yesterday how it had gone, but I was so anxious to get you to come out with me again, that I forgot. So I meant to ask first thing tonight, but then I saw you and everything else just sort of melted away."

Dani could feel her cheeks warming, and it had nothing to do with the last remnants of the sun. She decided to ignore the hopelessly mushy sentence and instead, answered, "They had a boy. Carson Sinclair. I'm looking forward to playing the role of benevolent aunt. I want to be the kind who keeps forbidden snacks at the house for the taking. The kind of aunt who allows the kids to spend the night and stay up as late as they want. The one who takes them to the zoo, to the park, shopping when they're older."

"You've given this a lot of thought." He chuckled, then reached out casually and put his hand on hers.

She glanced down at them, positioned on the picnic table. They looked right together.

"I . . ." Where was she? Oh, the baby. "I've been planning it since Connie called and said she was pregnant. That's one of the reasons I jumped at the job offer from Hamlin. Being able to be close to my family, to be here when the baby was born and have a chance to be that favorite aunt on a regular basis, and not just on the occasional holiday, those were big factors in my decision. Not that getting a chance to head things up, to really show what I can do was secondary."

"So you think you'll be staying?"

Dani nodded. "Unless I totally tank at the job, yes. I mean, New York was an exciting place to live, and I so look forward to going back to visit, but Erie's home."

They sat, side by side on the picnic bench, watching as the sun moved closer and closer to the water at the horizon.

Luke broke the silence by asking, "Are things any better at work?"

"Maybe. But there's still something there, and I've yet to figure out what it is."

"I'm sure you will."

They lapsed back into silence, but as they watched the sun sink below the horizon, Luke stroked her hand softly. It was a simple gesture, but it somehow served as a balm after the oddness the previous week.

When all that was left of the sunset was the rose colored afterglow, Luke stood. "We probably should head back to the car. The park closes after sunset."

"It wouldn't look good if we got busted by the cops," she teased.

"Two prominent Erie business people out on the beach after dark. The press would have a field day."

"We'd need dark sunglasses to avoid them," she added, getting into the spirt of things.

"Getaway vehicles to escape the paparazzi."

"Lawyers."

"Of course."

They lapsed into a comfortable silence after the silliness and Dani watched the last few pink rays fade.

Luke took her hand and gently pulled her up from the bench. "This was nice."

"Very nice. We've officially made it through a date without my brother or parents busting in. Or you being called away by some work-related emergency."

"Don't jinx us," he warned. "I never was a believer in superstitions, but you've made me a convert."

"Well, I'm afraid I need to get home, so tonight's date is just about over. There's not a lot to jinx."

"You have to get back right away? I mean, I'm sure we could find something else to do."

"Sorry. I'd like to, really, but I've got a ton to do. I'm heading out of town on Saturday. I'll be back next Monday. I thought I'd stop by the club on Thursday, if that's alright with you."

A shadow passed over his face, but was gone so fast, Dani wondered if she'd really seen it at all. Maybe she was looking for trouble.

When he smiled and said, "That would be great. I'm sure Sherri will want to fill you in on her date," she felt a surge of relief.

"Great. I've been working on some new stuff. I have this orange notebook I carry with me all day, jotting down ideas whenever they occur. To be honest, it's more of a journal, but there's a lot of fodder for comedy in my life. I'm anxious to try some of it out."

He paused a moment, then nodded. "Great. Thursday then. It's a date."

They drove home in silence. It wasn't quite as comfortable as it had been when they watched the sun set.

Luke pulled up in front of her house and left the motor running. For a moment, she didn't think he was going to get out. But just as she was about to open her door, say goodnight and just go in, he turned the key.

"I'll walk you to the door."

He came around and opened her car door for her. "Luke, is something wrong? I mean, after the other night and. . . . I mean, I think things are going well between us, but maybe I'm wrong."

He wrapped an arm over her shoulder as they walked toward her door. "You're not wrong. I think so, too. Something happened the first time we met, a spark."

"You sparked over a woman scraping bug guts from her shoe?"

"Killer-bug guts. It sounds stupid if you don't add the killer."

She smiled as she heard her own words echoed back to her.

"And yes. There you were in your very spinstery-looking business suit, scraping your shoe, and I just knew you were something special. Here's something you didn't know. Chris didn't ask me to drive you to work. I caught a glimpse of you as I came in and asked about you. He filled me in and I volunteered to give you a ride."

"Why Mr. Miller, you dog you. Do you always pick up women at Chris's station?"

"I'll confess, I never felt the least bit of an inclination before that day."

They'd reached her apartment door. "I do have a lot to do, but maybe you could come in for a few minutes?"

"I'd like that."

She unlocked the door, her hands less steady than normal. She let them in, shut the door and without waiting to move beyond the apartment's entryway, she turned and kissed him. Kissed him long and hard.

"Wow," he said as they paused for breath. "What was that for?"

"That was for being you."

"Care to be more specific?"

"For sparking over me when I was dressed like a repressed nun with killer-bug guts over my shoe. For daring to go out with me after having my brother, then my parents interrupt our dates. For . . ." She shrugged. "For just being you. I've got to confess, you spark for me, too."

"I know you have work to do, but maybe we could continue our sparking somewhere more comfortable for a little bit?"

She looked at him and raised an eyebrow.

"Your living room, the couch," he clarified.

"That might be arranged. Of course, we'd have to clear the couch off."

She walked to the living room doorway and flipped up the light switch.

Luke stepped up next to her and surveyed the room. "Dani, it's been weeks and you still haven't unpacked?"

"I've unpacked a few boxes, the necessities. It's just I hit the ground running at work, and then Connie had the baby, and I'll confess, there's been a certain man who's eaten up a lot of my time. Even when I'm not with him, I'm thinking about him."

"That's nice to hear, since he's thought about you a lot as well. So much so, he forgot to place an order this week. But, thinking and time-constraints aside, you need to unpack."

"I agree."

"Then, let's clear a path from here to the couch. We have to empty every box that's on the way. Unpack it and put the contents away. Only then will we permit ourselves to do more spark-ing."

Dani laughed. "I predict this will be the fastest any boxes have ever been emptied."

Dani didn't think she'd ever unpacked any-thing quite so quick. The boxes in their way were mainly books that needed to be shelved, and extra linens that had to go in the closet.

"You take the linens, I'll start the books."

They joked and chatted as they worked. Yes, whatever had been bothering Luke seemed to have passed. Dani couldn't remember ever feel-ing the kind of rush she felt every time she looked his way. He was cute, but he wasn't des-tined for any underwear ads on Times Squares. He was an average, nice looking man, who ran a business. He had a ready smile, and a sense of humor.

The thing was, Dani had worked with, and

even dated a lot of men who fit that description. Intelligent, articulate, funny, nice looking.

So, what was it that set Luke apart from the rest? That had her stomach tied in knots?

They'd unpacked all the designated boxes and she hadn't come up with any answers.

"So, the couch is now officially empty," Luke said, with a grin and an eyebrow wiggle that she assumed was supposed to look sexy and inviting, but just looked cute, which was all the inviting she needed.

"Why, I do believe you're right."

"Maybe we should sit on it and see if having all those boxes piled on it damaged the springs."

"Well, it wouldn't do to have guests sit on it if there were springs sticking out. It's a matter of safety."

"Yes. You never who might get the sue-happy fever and take you to court over a spring in the backside."

"Thank you, Luke for looking out for my welfare."

"My pleasure."

She sat down and bounced for good measure. "I'm happy to report this side is spring-free."

He sat on the opposite end and did the same. "Same here."

"All that leaves is the middle."

"We'd better be thorough and check it as well."

They both slid over a bit until they were touching. Thigh to thigh. Arm against arm. At least until he put his arm over her shoulders and pulled her even closer.

"It seems fine here," she assured him.

"Here, too, except for one thing."

"Oh?" she asked.

"It's a bit lonely."

She laughed. She seemed to do a lot of that when she was with Luke, and it had nothing to do with the fact they spent so much of their time together in his club.

"I guess I can figure out how to rectify that loneliness," she said, turning toward him and slipping her hands onto his shoulders, nudging his face towards her, bringing his lips to hers.

She'd barely gotten a taste of his lips when the doorbell rang. She glanced at her watch. "It's nine o'clock at night. Who could that be?"

"Only one way to find out."

She hurried to the door, anxious to find out who it was and send them on their way. "Mart."

"I talked to Henry today. He said you had a publishing emergency last night and sent someone named Sherri to break the news to him."

"Sorry. You know how busy starting a new job can be. I still haven't even managed to unpack."

Even though they'd cleared up a few boxes, there were still plenty and she gestured at them, just in case Mart hadn't noticed.

"Dani." He gave her the big-brother look. The same look he'd given her when he'd found out she'd gone out with Doug Matthews her freshman year.

Doug had been a senior. He was a wild, spent-more-time-in-detention-than-in-a-classroom sort of guy. And Mart had been less than happy when he found out about their date, and had given her the look. The same look he'd given when she'd told him she'd only applied to out-of-town colleges.

It was a look that said he didn't understand her and it was making him crazy.

"I'm sorry. It's just that regifting your blind-dates is going so well. I'm betting Henry liked Sherri, didn't he?"

"He was practically swooning." There was disgruntled disgust in Mart's voice. It was mixed with more than a touch of confusion.

"We have something going here, big brother. Some innate ability to match-make our friends."

"I don't want to find men for your colleagues and friends. I want to find someone for you."

Luke chose that precise moment to come out of the living room and into the foyer. It was a movie worthy entrance. And his line, "Sorry, she's already spoken for," was delivered with an Oscar-winning sense of timing.

"Miller," Mart said by way of greeting.

"Sinclair."

Both men stood quietly a moment, assessing each other in that caveman, chest-thumping, I'm-the-man sort of way that set Dani's teeth on edge.

Luke broke the heavy silence with, "I hear congratulations are in order." He extended his hand.

For a moment, Dani didn't think Mart was going to take it, but just as she was about to say something, he did.

"So, you're a comic?"

"I own the club. You?"

"Architect. Steelers, Browns or Bills?" Mart shot back.

Erie was a city divided by its football loyalties. It was within two hours driving time of Pittsburgh, Cleveland and Buffalo. The community was split three-ways, each faction ardent in its support for their 'hometeam.'

"Steelers. You?"

Mart answered with a man slap on the shoulder. "How about the Superbowl in '06? I about had a heart attack."

"I was in Denver at the stadium for the play-offs. They were nosebleed seats, but still."

"Get out," Mart said, obviously impressed.

They moved along the recently cleared path to the equally recently cleared couch, still rhapsodizing about their team. Names like Hines Ward and Jerome Bettis were bandied about, along with play-by-play recaps of various games from the last decade or so.

An hour later, a phone call from Connie broke up the manly bonding. Reluctantly, Mart got up. Dani walked him to the door. He leaned down, kissed her cheek and whispered, "I'm man enough to admit I was wrong. He's a good guy."

"Because he cheers for the right team?" she teased.

"No. Because he not only made it through Mom and Dad's crashing in on your dinner, but the whole time I grilled him, he couldn't take his eyes off you. He humored me, but couldn't wait to be with you."

"I still think it's because he liked the Steelers. You know you bleed black and gold."

"I'll admit, that didn't hurt."

He was laughing as he left, and Dani returned to the living room, shaking her head. "You passed."

"I know. I thought it would be work, but turns out, your brother's as nice as the rest of your family. Plus, he's a Steeler fan." He said the words as if it meant everything, as if being a Steeler fan gave him the measure of her brother.

"Men," she said, but she couldn't really muster much ire. As a matter of fact, she was pretty sure she was grinning.

"It's getting late and you have to work tomorrow. I probably should be going, too." He stood, but she could see his reluctance to end the evening.

She echoed that reluctance. "Sorry our evening was interrupted, once again, by my family." She followed him to the front door.

"That's okay," he assured her. "I think I've won them all over. Well, except your sister-in-law."

"There's no winning there. She'll love you because I," Dani caught herself and finished, "because I like you."

But what she'd almost said was, *she'll love you because I love you.* And that was absolutely absurd. She hardly knew Luke. She'd never been one to believe that love came easy. It took a long time to build, layer upon layer of connections. And yet, the words had almost tripped easily from her mouth.

Love him?

Did she?

Could she?

Her head was spinning with the question as they said their goodbyes. Luke gave her a kiss goodbye at the doorway that she knew would feature heavily in her dreams. "Wow."

"Call you tomorrow?" he asked.

"Yes. And see you Thursday."

His smile slipped a notch, but he nodded. "Can't wait. Oh, and before I go, Sherri had an idea for Friday night . . ."

From the Comedy Journals of Dani Sinclair:

I saw a T-shirt that read, Life's a Beach. I have to concur. Like a beach, sometimes life is like the sand, blistering hot and sizzling you right down to your very toes. Sometimes it's cool and soothing like the water, washing over you and carrying you away.

And sometimes, well, sometimes it's a great big seagull pooping on you.

If you're lucky, a good trip to the beach includes all three. Just like life. You walk across the heat to get to that cool water. And you have to be fast about it in order to dodge the seagull poop.

That wasn't very funny.

I know this is supposed to be funny, but

analyzing my feelings for Luke doesn't feel very laugh-worthy.

Trying to sort out those feelings, hot, cool and soothing . . . well, the sorting is the bird poop.

Chapter Ten
In the Spotlight

Over the next few days, Dani felt she'd made some inroads on both her relationship with Luke and with her stand-up.

Not so much on the sorting out and defining her feelings for him. She felt as if she was still jumbled and tumbled about them.

Not so much on the unpacking situation. Her house was still filled with boxes.

And definitely not so much on the job situation.

Oh, the business side of the job seemed to be on track. She'd gone through old records and felt she had a handle on how things had been done under the old administration. She felt that was an important understand where the company was coming from in order to formulate solid plans on ways to improve the efficiency and the product, while keeping their costs down.

She was pretty sure her plans were going to make a difference in not only the bottom line, but in the quality of the product. Most exciting of all, in her opinion, was the idea of taking versions of textbooks to eFormat. She felt a sense of certainty that eBooks were going to be the wave of the future and she wanted Hamlin to be on of the first on that particular bandwagon.

Sometime in the next few weeks she wanted to start an exploration committee. She had meetings scheduled with a couple firms who were cutting edge in the technology for eBooks while she was in New York.

When she'd taken the job, the board of directors had advocated firing staff. Oh, they'd referred to it as laying off employees, but Dani knew there would be no rehiring, which in her mind made it firing. She was adamantly opposed to it, and because they'd granted her autonomy, at least for six months, she'd kept everyone on, despite the fact they were all still the strangest, the most nervous group of people she'd ever worked with.

The bad news was, she hadn't been able to set their minds at ease over whatever was troubling them. Heck, she hadn't even been able to work out what was troubling them.

The good news was, she'd worked out a new routine for her stand-up. No family stories, no single-girl in the city. Too many comics used those as a basis for their acts. Dani had been searching for her schtick, something that would set her apart from everyone else. She was pretty sure the office had given her just that.

She was busy perfecting her corporate comic bits. She'd been working on it, new comic sketches that dealt with the corporate life. Stories, she hoped, would appeal to people outside the business, as well as insiders. From climbing up the corporate ladder, to reaching a top position and realizing that going to work was still a job and all the top meant is she had so much further to fall than she used to.

She'd tried out bits and pieces, but tonight, she was going to try out the whole act. And if she didn't fall flat on her face, she was going to do it on Friday night as a warm-up for the opening act, who would warm-up the audience for tonight's headliner.

She was the warm-up's warm-up.

Sherri had suggested it, and had lobbied Luke into let her try. He'd seemed less than enthused, though he'd grudgingly agreed.

Dani was determined to do well, to show him his faith in her wasn't misplaced.

That's why Thursday night was so important.

It was her last opportunity to work on polishing her act before her big Friday night debut.

Luke was tied up with some delivery man, and Dani found herself backstage talking to WLVH's morning DJ's Punch and Judy.

". . . and they fell in love in that truck. The station is starting to get quite the reputation as a place—"

Punch, who was in actuality Parker, interrupted his wife. "Don't say it." He turned to Dani and added in a stage-whisper, "My wife is a hopeless romantic."

"WLVH is getting a reputation," she repeated, smiling at him with a stubborn sort of smile, "as a place *where love is more than just a song* is more than our motto, it's our way of life."

Punch just groaned. "Bently, you've got a sick, sick sense of romance."

"I can prove it. There was Mary and Ethan." She clicked the couple off on a finger. "Then there was us." Another finger clicked up. "And Cassie and Cooper." The third one. "Even Ted." Number four.

"Ted," Parker scoffed. "Whoever thought he'd go all gooey-eyed?"

"I did. So did Cassie, at least when she got over being mad at Ted." A fifth finger flew up. "And Craig. Craig's going to pop the question any day now."

Parker just groaned.

Judy laughed. "Hey, with all the time WLVH has been spending here, you'd better be careful. Love has a way of happening whenever we're around."

"I . . ." Dani didn't know what to say to that, so she opted to say nothing, which made Judy laugh even harder.

"You can't win," Punch told her. "Don't even try."

"Punch and Judy, time to go," Sherri said. "You're up first," she told Dani.

Love is in the air?

Luke came backstage and smiled at her. And for a moment, for just that one moment, all her sorting and worrying about what her feelings were evaporated.

"You get everything straightened out?" she asked, wondering how it was he couldn't sense the way her heart had sped up, the way her very body seemed to warm whenever he walked into a room . . . or back stage, as the case may be.

"I think so. I'd like to have just one quiet night where everything went the way it was supposed to."

"I don't mind the chaos."

He looked as if he didn't quite believe her.

"Really. I just like being with you."

His smile was even broader as he took her hand. "And I—"

". . . Dani Sinclair," Judy called from onstage.

He dropped her hand. "Break a leg." He was still smiling, but this time didn't quite reach his eyes.

Dani thought about Punch and Judy's joking about WLVH's recent track record where love was concerned. She didn't know all the people they'd mentioned, but she could see their sincerity. Well, Judy's sincerity.

Loving Luke? He still wouldn't talk to her. One moment they seemed as close as could be, then the next, he'd pull back.

If he wouldn't talk to her, would they have a chance? Loving Luke might not be enough. If it were true, would more than her leg be broken?

She made her way to center stage, her feelings a jumbled mess. But as she stood in front of the microphone, all those worries fell away. "How's everyone tonight?" Answering murmurs rippled through the crowd.

She smiled. "I'm glad you're all having a good night. I'm hoping tonight is better for me than the rest of the week has been."

She waited a pregnant moment then teasingly scolded, "This is where you ask me what happened the rest of the week?"

A voice obligingly called out the question.

"Thank you. And I'll tell you what happened. You might not be able to tell, but I work in corporate America. Business. CEO in fact. But I don't know if I've quite got the hang of it. You see . . ."

Dani was getting better on stage.

Much better.

Last night had proven just how much better. It had been her last Thursday night amateur night before this evening's big event. Having Dani serve as the warm-up acts warm-up had been Sherri's idea.

Luke wished he felt better about her doing it. But he didn't.

Dani was a natural, and she was improving each time she got center stage.

And Luke was getting more and more disgusted with himself. He should be happy for her. And he knew, intellectually at least, that she wasn't anything like his ex.

And yet knowing that and feeling that were two different things.

He forced a smile as he walked back Friday night.

He kissed her cheek and she looked so pleased to see him, he hugged her as well, and couldn't help but notice how very stiff she seemed. "Problems?"

"There are a lot more people here on a Friday night than on Thursdays. I knew that. I mean, I've been here on weekends and know you pretty much fill every seat, but . . ." She moved the curtain aside and peeked out again. "I never knew it from this angle. From backstage. It looks worse."

"Weekends are always packed. That's why I do amateurs on Thursdays. They come in, bring their families and fill the seats on what would otherwise be a fairly dead night."

"Yes, I know that. You've told me that. But it seems everything I know, everything I've ever known is gone. All that's left is—" she peeked out the curtain again, "them."

Luke said, "Turn around. What you can't see you can't worry about."

She looked at him and he made a twirling motion with his finger, and she complied. He started to rub her rock-hard muscles in her shoulder. "Take a deep breath. You're going to be fine."

"I can't remember one line, one story, not one part of my act."

Part of Luke, the part he was ashamed of, wanted to say, *So just forget it. Walk away. You don't have to do this, don't have to prove anything.*

Another part wanted to tell her about his ex.

How she'd admitted, as she packed to leave, that the only reason she'd dated him was to get a break. She'd wanted to meet other comics, wanted to learn. That's why she sought him out and dated him.

And she did. When she'd learned enough, she'd packed and left. But not before he'd become fodder for a new bit. When she'd started in on, "I know they say that women are the sentimental ones in a relationship, but that's not necessarily true. Why, this guy . . ."

Things he'd thought were thoughtful, she ridiculed and turned into a comedy sketch. Luke might have let that go and just chalked it up to comedic poetic licence. After all, he had thought he'd loved her. And he'd thought she loved him. But when she left, he'd realized he'd been played for a fool.

Every comedic zing cut, every remembered moment, stung. And though he knew deep-down that Dani wasn't doing that, he couldn't seem to help feeling threatened every time she got up on stage. He waited for her to use him as the focus of her bit.

But she hadn't.

At least not yet.

But each time, he waited. He knew his reaction wasn't fair and was determined to tell her, explain to her.

Tonight.

After this set, he'd tell her. He'd get it out in the open and maybe then he could put it behind him. Because Dani wasn't Caitlyn. Even when she talked about people she knew in her act, she was never brutal, never mean.

Plus, she wasn't a real comic. This was just a hobby. She had a job at Hamlin. She had family here in Erie. She wasn't going to walk away.

He forced himself to be supportive, knowing by now that Dani tended to get stage-fright right before she went on. He also knew that the moment she hit center stage and got in front of that microphone, she forgot all about it. She loved being there.

And even though it made him feel low, he hated that she loved it.

Her head was stuck between the gap in the curtain. "There are more people coming in."

He snapped the curtain back in place. "No more peeking. You're only going to make yourself more nervous."

"I don't think being more nervous is possible. My stomach is eating itself, churning acid as if it were getting paid for it. My legs are watery and I'm sweating. No perspiring, or glowing, but sweating. I don't think I can do this."

Luke knew the feeling she was talking about. He had the same feeling when he thought about talking to her tonight. "What you have to do is give yourself something else to think about."

"Like what?" she countered.

"Something at work?"

"I come here to forget about work. Everyone there is still . . . well, off." She shrugged. "I don't know why, what I'm doing, so I don't have a clue how to fix it. I've called meetings, both group and private, but all I get is that everything's alright, that everyone loves their jobs. Coming here, doing my bit, is my pressure valve."

"How's that going for you tonight?" he asked, grinning. Feeling relief wash through him as he was reminded this was Dani's avocation, not her vocation.

"Not so good."

"Okay, don't think about work. How's your sister-in-law doing?"

"The baby has colic, so there have been a lot of frantic phone calls flying back and forth between the worried mom and dad, my parents and the doctor."

"More tension." He put his arm over her shoulder and pulled her close.

"And before you suggest it, I'd prefer not thinking about killer bugs." It was the first all-out, no-mistake-about-it smile he'd seen her wear tonight. "It might be distracting, but it's still embarrassing."

"Well, you've tied my hands. There's only one thing left to do."

"Oh?"

He pulled her closer. "Remember this is just in the interest of calming you down. I consider it my obligation as club owner to soothe my comics."

He kissed her. And while his lips were on hers, drinking her in, he forgot all about his worries, all about the fact she'd be on stage soon. He forgot there'd ever been a woman named Caitlyn.

All he could think about, all he could focus on was this . . . was Dani. Was how right it felt to be with her like this. The kiss ended and he pulled her into a tight hug.

"This is supposed to calm me down?" Her voice was breathless against his shoulder.

"Well, maybe that's the wrong turn of phrase. But it is supposed to distract you." And because he couldn't help himself, he leaned down and kissed her again. It was just as earth-shattering and universe altering as the last one.

"Is it working?" he asked.

"What people?" she countered, grinning. "But maybe we should do it again. I'm starting to remember there's a crowd out front."

"We can't have that." As he kissed her, Luke realized how foolish he was. Dani was nothing like his ex. She might enjoy being on stage, but her kiss said she liked him more.

Yes, it was long past time to talk to her, to lay it all out on the line. To tell her he was pretty sure what they had was something deeper than just a dating relationship. What he felt for her was—

"Ten minutes," Sherri called, cutting off his train of thought and breaking up the kiss.

Reluctantly, Dani pulled back. "Thanks, I need that."

"Always happy to oblige," he assured her, grinning because something had changed. The knot that had been in his stomach every time Dani went on stage had loosened. "When you're done here, I'd like to talk. There are a few things I've been wanting to tell you."

"Anytime, you know that. And while you're telling me things, tell me that's not your method for soothing all your nervous comics."

"No, only the very special ones."

Before he could stop her, Dani reached for the curtain and pulled it back. He could almost see every one of her muscles tense back up.

"It's a full house," she whispered. "I don't think there's ever been more than half on open-mic night."

Luke started tugging her back, but not before every ounce of color faded from her face. "Oh, no."

He finally managed to pry her hands from the curtain and pull her back. "Dani?"

"I can't go on."

"Dani?"

"I won't do it. I won't go on."

Luke flashed back to the last night Caitlyn had been scheduled at Chuckles. *"I won't do it,"* she'd told him. *"I just signed a contract, and I'll be working clubs that actually pay me. I won't do another amateur night at your two-bit club."*

She'd gone on to tell him in great detail how she'd used him, that she'd always known Chuckles was nothing more than a stepping stone to bigger and better things.

That *he* had been nothing more than a stepping stone.

Each word in her tirade had cut at him. He'd loved her, or at least thought he loved her.

In retrospect the words didn't cut quite so deep. Was it time? Or was it Dani?

He wasn't sure.

Earlier, holding Dani, he couldn't imagine feeling that way about anyone but her.

"Dani, come on, you've done this before. There's just a few more people out there than you're used to."

"I can't. I won't."

Her words echoed Caitlyn's. Luke's jaws clenched. His stomach churned raw acid.

"Luke, I won't go on. There—"

"Dani, this little temper tantrum isn't like you?"

"Temper tantrum?"

He realized he hadn't chosen the most diplomatic phrasing. "Listen, I know this is a hobby for you, but for me, it's my business, my livelihood. I can't let your hysterics stop the show." He knew, even as acid bubbled in his stomach, that this wasn't about Dani, it was his issue. But unfortunately, knowing and feeling were two different things. He needed to hold back his anger, but he was doing a piss poor job of it. "You're not behaving professionally."

"That's the point, isn't it? I'm not a professional. I'm an amateur. I don't get paid. This is just for fun. Well, it's not fun tonight and I'm telling you, I can't do this."

"Dani, don't go playing prima dona with me. Nerves or not, you've got five minutes—"

"I don't because I'm not going on. Let me explain."

"You don't need to explain. I didn't want to do this, have you on tonight. But Sherri convinced me that you've got talent, that I should give you a shot. But you're too big for my club, aren't you? What are you holding out for? Money? Do you think you're ready to take on bigger venues? You're good, but you're not that good."

"Luke, I'm sorry, but—"

He simply held up a hand. "Whatever. If

you're not going on, then I'd better go make some plans. Because this might be a game for you, a stepping-stone, but Chuckles is my livelihood."

"Luke . . ."

He didn't stay to hear what she said. He simply left, damning himself for a fool as he stomped off. He'd thought Dani was different, but she wasn't. She didn't take her commitment to his club seriously. She didn't honor her obligations.

She was just like Caitlyn, using him and his club until they were no longer useful.

As Luke walked away, Dani was just left standing there wondering what to do next. Should she stay or go?

When he came back his face was closed, no expression she could read.

"I guess I'll be going now. But later, I'd like to explain."

"Go ahead, go. Do what you have to. And don't worry about explanations, I get it."

"Luke—" she started.

He cut her off. "I'm busy. This is my business, and you're leaving me scrambling."

"And I'm sorry. I'd really like to talk to you later."

"Whatever."

Dani left through the back door, confused by Luke's reaction. Confused by her own.

Michelle and Allie from work had been sitting in the audience. What were the odds they'd be here tonight?

Maybe she should have gone on anyway. But she'd never done her gig in front of people she knew. Luke and Sherri didn't count.

But doing her act in front of two employees? Doing new material that was gleaned from her work at Hamlin?

People were already behaving so strangely at work, she felt she had to maintain some degree of professionalism, and standing up, center stage, and poking fun at the business world, specifically, publishing, didn't seem like quite the way to go to put them at ease.

She wanted to explain that to Luke, wanted him to understand, but he didn't seem in the mood to listen.

One moment they'd been kissing and he'd been sweet, the next?

Dani got into her car and drove away from Chuckles, wondering if she'd ruined things for good.

Luke might own a comedy club, but he took his business as seriously as she took hers, and she'd let him down.

Feeling anything but funny, Dani drove toward home.

She'd moved home so full of ideas and excitement. A new challenging job, being close to her family. And then, the first day on her way to work she'd met Luke, and thought that maybe finally she'd found a relationship like her parents had, like Mart and Connie had.

All that optimism, all those plans.

Nothing had gone the way she'd hoped.

Her family still thought of her as a little girl, work was still odd, and Luke?

Her relationship with him wasn't going the way she'd hoped it would.

Luke watched Dani go still riding a red-hot anger. She'd made the club look bad. Made him look bad.

But by the time the opening act finished that red-hot feeling had died to a cold ball in the pit of his stomach.

He felt like a heel. A first-class jerk. And though he'd had to scramble, finding someone to take over the opening wasn't tough. One of his regulars was in the audience and had agreed. Having local talent open for the opening act of a big-name draw was a long-standing tradition.

No, having Dani back out wasn't nearly as big a deal as he'd made out. And he wasn't mad at her, though he was sure she'd never believe it. It took him that first act to figure out what that spike of anger had been about. And when the answer hit him, he felt lower than low.

That anger had covered his relief. Relief that Dani wasn't going on stage, wasn't taking that one small step away from total amateur. And that relief disgusted him. His anger was all directed at himself, though he was pretty sure that Dani wouldn't believe that either.

Sherri came back, frowning. "What did you do?"

"Nothing. She got cold feet when she saw the full house and left."

"And?"

"Okay, so maybe I wasn't overly sympathetic."

"But you didn't want her to do it in the first place."

"I know, it doesn't make sense, but I guess men are as entitled to a bit of irrationality as any woman is."

"That was sexist, and I'm not even going to go there. I am going to remind you again that she's not—"

She didn't have to finish. Luke interrupted. "I know. But knowing and feeling . . ."

"Two different things. You still haven't told her, have you?"

"No."

"Tell her. Explain. Then grovel. A lot."

"I—"

"No more time. We've got to start."

"You know, one day you're going to have to acknowledge that I'm the boss and you're the employee."

Sherri laughed. "I know I tell you that you're not funny and should avoid the stage, but maybe I was wrong 'cause that was quite funny."

"I'm going to dock your check."

Sherri laughed even harder. "Funny, funny man."

Luke shook his head. He would never understand women, but maybe that was alright, because the way things were looking, he was never going to understand himself either.

Dani looked at the boxes that still lined the walls of her living and dining rooms. She had an unexpected evening off. She could probably make some inroads at unpacking, but she couldn't seem to work up any enthusiasm for it.

Instead she curled on the couch, wishing she had her favorite afghan to wrap up in, but it was in one of the boxes she couldn't find the energy to unpack, so she did without.

She wasn't sure just where she'd gone wrong. She'd so enjoyed doing her stand-up, but when she'd seen Allie and Michelle in the audience, two employees, she realized she couldn't go on.

She was their boss. A young boss. She'd spent the last weeks trying to show everyone at Hamlin that she was capable, trying to build a reputation. Playing at comic certainly wouldn't enhance that reputation at all.

Stand-up was a fun hobby, but publishing was her job. A job she loved. She wasn't going to risk it on something frivolous.

Maybe she should have tried harder to make Luke understand, but to be honest, he'd been in a less than understanding mood of late.

Since she'd moved back home, she'd managed to screw up a relationship and a fun hobby. There was no way she was going to screw up her job.

Rather than unpacking, she got up and began to pack. She was leaving town tomorrow. When she got back next week, she was going to do what she'd planned when she first got to town. She was going to concentrate on work and forget anything that distracted her from that.

That included Luke Miller and her short lived amateur career as a comic.

Danielle Sinclair was a woman on a mission.

From the Comedy Journals of Dani Sinclair:

I think we all have a need to be in the spotlight.

We have this old family video my father

took. My brother had built this elaborate model of a building he'd designed for a school project. He was explaining all the bits and what-nots. I was about four, and didn't like being upstaged even then. Dad, dad, dad, dad, tape me, I kept chanting. He'd turn the camera on me, and tell me to go ahead. I stood there, frozen, not sure what to do now that I had what I wanted— the spotlight.

When my dad finally turned the camera on me that day, the only thing my four-year-old mind could come up with to compete with my brother's building project was, "My teacher says a pregnant goldfish is called a twit."

This definitely isn't a comedy routine. It's my life. Right now, I feel like a twit for thinking Luke and I might have something special.

Chapter Eleven
Home Is Where the Heart Is
and Other Urban Legends

For years, New York City had been home, but even though her business trip back was a success, something had changed.

Dani took a meeting on Saturday afternoon with a manufacturer of a new eBook Readers. Afterward she spent a couple hours walking around the New York streets before meeting with friends for an evening out on the town. Dinner at their favorite hangout, and then they saw *Wicked*. The show was fantastic, and for those few hours, she was able to forget her worries.

Being in New York should have been a coming home. She drank in the city and at first she couldn't remember why it was she'd gotten sick of it. The lights, the hustle and bustle, even the smell of being back in a Broadway theater.

It was all so big, so vibrant. She missed it and practically waxed poetic about the virtues of the city to her friends who laughed and urged her to come back.

After she'd said her goodbyes, she'd gone back to the hotel and sat in the window, looking out at the street, watching the people hurry past. Why had she ever left? The question kept plaguing her.

Why had she gone back to Erie, to a job where everyone still treated her as an outsider, to a family who would never learn to see her as an adult? Back home to a brother who didn't think she could even manage picking her own dates.

For the life of her, she couldn't remember why moving to Erie had seemed like such a good idea when New York had everything she could want. Sitting in the theater, watching the show had been wonderful.

Mart had told her Erie's theater life was strong and growing. The Warner Theater, on State Street, attracted touring shows. She'd already reserved two seats for next season. She'd thought she'd invite Luke, but that didn't seem likely.

She'd hoped he'd call, but he hadn't. She knew weekends at the club were crazy for him, and tried to make excuses. But all her excuses were sounding lame to her own ears.

She'd kept her cell phone on high, just in case he called. She'd check it frequently, despite her best intentions. There was still no call on Sunday, or Monday.

As her plane took off on Tuesday and she watched the city fade from sight, she felt a pang of loss and very little sense of excitement at going back home to her job, to watching her relationship with Luke fade away. She'd run out of excuses for him.

Though the trip had been a success, it was about the only positive thing in her life at the moment.

But as the plane circled the bay, banking and turning for its approach to the runway, she spotted the Bicentennial Tower at the end of the dock, all lit up. It had been built after she'd left for school, but it had already become a landmark. That tower at the end of the dock said Erie.

Dani saw it and waited for that warm sense of coming home to flood through her body, but it didn't come. She'd felt it in New York. Maybe this whole move had been a mistake. She felt as if she didn't know where she belonged, where to call home. She felt displaced.

The feeling didn't abate as she disembarked and collected her luggage.

She got to her car and jabbed at the button for

the radio, hoping the noise would help fill up the hollow feeling.

"This is Cassie and you've tuned into Night Calls, here on WLVH, where love is just a song. I have Anna on the phone. Anna?"

"Hi, Cassie. I've got a problem. There's this guy in my biology class. I think he likes me, but he's shy. I don't mind asking him out, but how can I tell if he'll be receptive?"

"You never can tell for sure. I've always found the best thing is to be direct. Don't beat around the bush and play games. If you want to know where you stand, ask. And here is an old song by Cher, suggesting that the way to really tell what a man feels is with a kiss."

Cher, singing the Shoop-Shoop song.

Great. Part of Dani wanted to turn off the song. After all, the kissing part wasn't the problem with Luke. The running hot, running cold part was. She wasn't sure where she stood, and if she was someone who took radio DJ's advice to heart, she'd just ask him.

Part of her wanted to do just that. Ask. Get an answer and move on.

The other part was afraid of what his answer would be.

She drove back to her house, to the myriad of unpacked boxes and wondered if she should bother unpacking at all.

Maybe this move had been a mistake. Maybe it was time to cut her losses and admit this wasn't working out. Things hadn't gotten any better at work. Everyone still acted as if she had a plague. Afraid to come too close, that whatever it was she had was catching.

The only bright point was little Carson. Her mother and father were enjoying their new role as grandparents extraordinaire. Mart and Connie were beaming, in a totally exhausted and overwhelmed sort of way.

If she left, if she called this quits, she'd miss out on watching her nephew grow. Oh, she'd come home for visits, for holidays, but she wouldn't be Aunt Dani, someone her nephew would really know, could count on.

For the first time in a long time, Dani was totally lost. She didn't know what to do, what direction to turn. Stay, leave? She'd come home to Erie with such high hopes for the company, for building a new chapter of her life.

Before she'd gone to work in the educational text market, she'd worked as a fiction editor for one of the bigger New York houses. Every editor had to spend time in the slush pile, picking through submissions. She'd read a lot of proposals that sounded like great ideas in the synopsis, the brief outline of the complete book. They appeared to have it all. Great characters, a good plot. Then she'd open up the sample chapters, filled with excitement, so sure she'd found something wonderful, only to discover what sounded so good in an outline lost something in the execution.

That's pretty much summarized her life right now. Moving home, taking the job at Hamlin, even playing at stand-up and casually dating Luke—it had all sounded great in theory. But as she was getting to the meat of it, it was falling flat. It was losing something in the execution.

Wednesday, she left her brother's house and returned to hers. She'd picked up a pizza from Patti's. The neighborhood store had been on Pine Avenue since she was at Mercyhurst Prep. A few years ago, they'd moved the store to a newer building across the street from its original location, but otherwise, the pizza was the same. Even some of the employees had been there since she was in school.

She opened the door to her apartment, hoping the warm, yeasty aroma would tempt some semblance of hunger, but all she could think about was crawling into her bed and going to sleep, but a light in the living room stopped her in the foyer.

"Hello?"

The minute she called out, she thought better of it. If it was a thief she could be in trouble. She set the pizza down on the nearest box, and opened the door, ready to bolt.

Her mother's face popped around the corner. "Good you're home. I expected you a long while back."

A surge of relief flooded her body.

"Mom, you scared me. I was ready to run out of the apartment and call 911."

"You gave me a key." She stepped into the entryway.

Dani didn't even bother to complain she hadn't seen her mother's car. The apartment's parking lot was large enough that unless she was specifically looking for a certain vehicle, or parked right next to it, she could easily miss anyone's car.

Dani's heart had finally slowed enough that she could concentrate on something other than breathing. And in this case, she concentrated on her mother, noting that she was wearing old clothes. "So, what are you doing here, Mom?"

"I never thought you'd get here," her mother said, not really answering the question. "Well, you're here now, and can give me a hand. But first you can offer me some of that pizza."

Her mother picked up the box and headed down the hall to the kitchen. "I've been working for the last few hours while I waited. I'm starving."

There was nothing left for Dani to do but follow. Her mother was opening a cupboard door. "Working at what?"

But as her mother pulled plates out and set them on the counter—plates Dani hadn't seen since the move—she had her answer.

"Unpacking, of course." She opened another cupboard door and took out two glasses. "You've been here far too long to be living out of boxes. It seems unsettled, as if you hadn't fully committed to your job, to staying here."

Dani felt a wave of guilt as her mother voiced what she'd been thinking for the last few days. "Mom, I don't think I have committed to staying. Going back to New York felt like going home. I waited for that feeling to hit me as we landed in Erie, and all I felt was tense. Things at work aren't going as well as I'd hoped they would, and—"

She stopped short, wanting to tell her mother about her problems with Luke, but not sure her mother wanted to hear about him.

"Your comic?" Her mother poured each of them a glass of wine—wine she must have brought with her because it hadn't been there when Dani left the house—and served them each a piece of pizza.

When Dani didn't answer, her mother prompted. "You're having problems with Luke?"

She sighed and took a sip from her glass. "That's not going at all well. I don't know what to make of him. One minute, things seem perfect, the next, not so much."

"So, you're thinking about just calling it quits with both your job and Luke?"

"You and dad encouraged me to pursue business and in business, you learn that sometimes you have to admit defeat. You have to know when to throw in the towel. These last few days, ever since I got home from New York, I've been wondering if moving back to Erie was the right idea."

"You're right," her mother agreed. "In business, there are times when you have to cut your losses and just let an idea go. But, Dani, this isn't business, it's your life. And in life, you have to know when to fight for what you want. You haven't given the job or the man enough of a chance."

"I can't figure out what's wrong with everyone at work, and no matter what I do, no one's talking. As for Luke, he's made himself clear. Whatever we were building is going to go further than it's gone. I can't make someone . . ." she hesitated, then finished, "care. They either do or they don't."

"I don't think that care is the word you wanted to use, but whatever you feel for him, you're right, you can't make him reciprocate, but you can insist on some answers. Make him talk to you, to tell you what's wrong. Maybe it's something fixable, maybe it's not. But you'll never know unless you ask. And as for work, you're the boss. You're in charge. If there's a problem, then it's your problem. Figure out what's what and fix it."

It sounded so easy when her mother said the words, but Dani knew that fixing things at work or with Luke wasn't that cut and dry. "But—"

Her mother held up a hand, stopping her. "Not if ands or buts about it. Fix your problems, don't run away. No matter how frustrated you are right now, Erie's your home. Your dad and I are here. Your brother, Connie and the baby are here. Fix things. And a good way to start fixing things is to declare yourself. Don't give yourself an out. Commit to staying. You can't do that if you're still living out of boxes."

"So, your suggestion is, all my problems can be solved by unpacking?"

Her mom laughed. "Maybe not solved, but it's a good place to start."

Dani drained her glass and then popped her last bite of pizza. "Okay, let's have at it."

"First, let's have another slice of pizza. I haven't had Patti's in a while, and it tastes even better than I remembered. I'm starving, and you might not think you are, but you haven't been eating right."

"Yes, mother," Dani said obediently, grinning.

"Now, that's what I like to hear."

Her mother brought the bottle of wine and the box of pizza to the table. And for the first time in a long time, since that first day at work, Dani felt a surge of excitement, a sense of possibility.

"Let's talk plans as we unpack. I'm sure, two resourceful women like us can come up with something. Luke and the people at your company don't stand a chance."

"Mom, before we start making plans, I want to tell you about something I've been doing since I moved home. A new hobby." She paused. "I've been doing stand-up."

Her mother laid a hand on Dani's and laughed. "Well, goodness knows this family provides plenty of fodder for an act."

"You don't mind?"

"Honey, you always loved the spotlight. So when can I come see you?"

Maybe, just maybe she could make this all work out.

Maybe Erie was where she belonged.

From the Comedy Journals of Dani Sinclair:

They say that home is where the heart is. I always thought it was an urban myth, rather like alligators in the sewer, and guys with hooks attacking kids making out in their car. You see, I left home to go to school and build a career, and though I love my family, my heart was in my education and in my job. I'd have sworn my heart was in New York, but coming back to Erie, to my family, I realized that maybe 'home is where the heart is' isn't quite the urban myth I thought it was. And if that's the case, I plan to be careful about those alligators and definitely won't be making out in the front seat of my boyfriend's car any time soon.

Of course, I'm not sure he's my boyfriend. But that's another comedy bit.

Chapter Twelve
Just Suck It Up

"**I**'ve called this meeting because . . ." Dani
had practiced what she wanted to say, how she
wanted to say it. She'd tried to convince herself
it was like being on stage, but doing a bit on stage
didn't seem nearly as intimidating as this did.

Her mother had helped her formulate a plan,
and last night as they unpacked, it had all sounded
sane and rational. Confronting the people here at
work, then facing Luke and demanding answers.

*You can't expect him to say the words if you're
afraid to.*

What words? she'd asked.

Her mother had just given her the mother-eye
and said, *Just suck it up and say the words. The
worst he can say is he doesn't feel the same.*

But before she dealt with Luke, she had to deal with work.

"I've asked some of you individually what, if anything is wrong, but no one's been able to tell me anything. And yet, there is something wrong. Something more than I'm a new boss. Something more than just my being young. You're all jumpy around me, acting as if at any moment I'm going to give you the axe, figuratively or literally. My assurances don't seem to help, nothing does."

No one said anything. They all watched her with all the nervousness of a mouse watching the cat. "We'll, we're not leaving here until I get some answers."

She didn't have anything else to say, couldn't think of any other way to compel them to talk to her, so she simply shut up and sat down.

Allie looked as if she might say something, and for a moment, Dani held her gaze, trying to will her to spill it, whatever it was. But Allie looked down, and Dani was forced to resign herself to the fact that she was going to have to wait it out. So, she settled comfortably back in her seat, picked up her pen and notebook and started writing.

You'd think being the boss would be great. Everyone has to listen to you. Your ideas can't be dismissed out of hand. When you talk, people listen.

But, there's a flipside, if your ideas suck, there's no one else to blame. And you can talk yourself blue in the face, but if you have nothing to say, then what?

Sometimes, you just have to sit back, and be quiet. Allow those who work with you to have a say, to find the idea. But that waiting for them can be hard.

Definitely no comedy in that. She tried again.

Bosses. Can't live with 'em, can't ignore them. Especially when you're the boss in question.

That was no better.

The stress and the strain of her job and relationship turmoil had robbed her of her ability to be funny. Even though her journal had long since stopped being just about comedy routines, this wasn't even good journaling.

She couldn't even imagine going on stage in this condition. She'd seen people tank on amateur night. And she didn't want to be one of those comics who got to the punchline and didn't even get a chuckle.

She stopped writing and looked out at the people in the silent meeting room. Allie, who on occasions seemed to be warming, to be less wary, and at others, seemed as nervous as ever.

As if on cue, Allie looked up and caught Dani's eye, before dropping her gaze.

Weird sayings, Dani scribbled. *Caught some-one's eye. Caught his eye. If you really think about it, that's just gross. Racing heart. Heart in your throat, foot in your mouth, ear to the ground* . . . What other sayings?

She mulled the idea around. Weird English turns of phrases. Yes, she could make a whole bit on that. It was funnier than her musings on being the boss. Ideas raced through her head. Actually, the absurdity of the English language had a lot of comic fodder for an act.

Not that she had any place to do stand-up anymore.

She missed being center stage, but if that was it, she'd cope. Unfortunately, she missed Luke more.

A lot more.

If this whole confrontation idea of her mother's worked here at work, could she figure out someway to reach Luke as well?

"Dani?"

She looked up. It was Allie. "Yes, Allie."

"It's . . ." Allie looked nervously from side to side, but everyone in her line of sight looked anywhere but at her. "Listen, it's the notebook."

"Notebook?"

"You've carried it everywhere with you, stopping whatever you're doing to write in it.

Everyone," murmurs from the rest of the crowd almost drowned her out. "Everyone, including myself, has mused about what you're writing in it. What kind of plans you're making for the company. More specifically, what those plans are going to mean to our jobs. You came in and promised no drastic changes until you learned the company. Well, you and the notebook have been here long enough to get the lay of the land, and we've all pretty much exhausted ourselves, living in uncertainty. It would be helpful if you would just tell us now."

"The orange notebook?"

"Yes."

Michelle stood up. "Every time we make a mistake, or there's a mishap, you pull it out and start scribbling. And every time we worry that you're keeping tally."

"We heard you were called the Terminator at Wellington," someone in the back called out.

"And we don't want to be terminated."

Dani stood, and laughed. Laughed harder than she'd laughed since leaving for New York. Everyone in the room watched her with hawk-like intensity, their nervousness apparent.

And that nervousness is what helped her finally settle down.

"I have a confession to make. I didn't start out a business major. I started out in the drama department. But my parents, after seeing me in a few plays, convinced me that my future was in another direction. They were right. I was never destined for a stage career, and I love what I do. But I've found a hobby, a way to have a bit of the spotlight, and still work at this job that I think I could learn to love. I've been doing some amateur stand-up. That's what the notebook is. Ideas for bits."

She paused and added, "To be honest, this entire transition has been as nerve wracking for me, as I imagine it has been for all of you. This," she tapped the journal, "was originally for comedy ideas, but it's morphed into more of a journal, my observations, not all of which are very funny."

More murmurs.

"I'll confess, the reason I started writing after any mishaps is . . . well, it was fodder for the act. No names are mentioned and the facts are changed to protect the innocent but there it is, I'm billing myself as The Corporate Comic, centering my act around the funny side of business. But listening to you all here, I realize that the more you acted weird around me, the more I wrote, and the more I wrote, the more nervous you became and acted weird and . . ." She laughed again. "It was a vicious circle."

"And the Terminator?" Allie asked.

"A friend where I used to work started that particular nickname because she said I could spot a typo a mile off. Anything that left my desk was pretty much error free. I wasn't in the position to terminate anything more than a dangling participle. And now that I can, I don't have any desire to. Your jobs are all safe. I have no plans in the immediate or distant future of firing anyone. I'm not promising that your job descriptions won't change, I'd like to streamline the editorial process, and . . . well, that can all wait until I have a firm plan to offer you. But I can't stress this strongly enough, you all are valuable assets. You're what makes Hamlin work. Your jobs are as safe as you want them to be."

No darting eyes, another good idea for the body-part bit—no frowns or nervous looks. Just a room full of smiles and contented murmurs. "I didn't think I wanted you all to know that I was doing stand-up, that it might make me seem less of a boss to you. And because I'm young, I didn't want to do anything that would remind you that I don't have much experience. I was wrong. Because, although I may be the boss, I'm also a person. I'd like to invite anyone who'd like to come, to be at Chuckles tomorrow night at seven. I'll be going on their open mic night."

"I'll be there," Allie assured her. "Me and Sam."

More promises were shouted.

Dani smiled, a plan beginning to take shape. She was going to play to her toughest crowd yet. And she wasn't referring to her coworkers, or her family, whom she planned to invite.

She was thinking about Luke Miller.

From the Comedy Journals of Dani Sinclair:

Just suck it up.

That was my mother's favorite retort for years.

When I was in high school, lamenting the fact that I had no chest to speak of. I mean, when my best friend looked down, she saw cleavage. I saw the floor. And I came to Mom for sympathy, but she basically told me to just suck it up.

I thought, at the time she was rather insensitive. But since then, I've come to find she's right.

There are certain things in life you can't change.

Not to be sexist or anything, but you'll never change the fact men don't put down toilet seats.

All you can do is suck it up and adjust to checking.

But there are things you can change.

For instance, I had this orange notebook at work that I wrote ideas for comedy bits in. It seems everyone worried about what I was writing, the more they worried, the more they goofed up, and I'd write it down, which would make them worry more and goof up more . . .

It was a vicious cycle. I couldn't figure out why they all walked on eggshells around me. But this was a situation I didn't just suck up . . . I asked. Things changed for the better.

Chapter Thirteen
Oh, Romeo

"Call her," Sherri said, not for the first time. Not for the fifteenth time either.

"I don't want to talk about this one the phone. I'm going to go see her on Monday."

"Why not today?"

"Because I'm going to need to grovel, and as a woman, I know that you know that groveling takes time. And you also know that time is in short order for me from Thursday through Saturday night."

"Grovel on Sunday?"

"No, I need to mentally prepare for my groveling. And since I'm busy for the next three days, there won't be time. My plan is to prepare on

Sunday, then hit her with a well-thought out apology, accompanied by plenty of groveling."

"Men are so dumb."

"Thanks."

"No, I mean it. You spend so much time thinking and worrying about what to say, that you don't realize we get it. You're not all Shakespeare. Just a simple I'm sorry, I was a jerk, is enough. We don't need, *Romeo, oh Romeo.*"

"Actually, odds are if I were trying to Shakespeare her into forgiving me, I wouldn't be shouting *Romeo*, I'd be going more for a Juliet quote."

"You know what I meant. You're just being argumentative because you know I'm right. You shouldn't wait."

"Monday."

"Men . . ." Whatever else Sherri had to say was lost as she walked away mumbling to herself. To be honest, he was pretty sure she didn't intend for him to hear. Sherri often said that the best conversation she had on any given day was with herself.

But despite his grousing, Luke knew he wanted nothing more than to call Dani, to hear her voice. He missed her. And he knew he'd behaved like a jerk. She deserved more than just a quick phone apology.

He just hadn't figured out what would suffice as an apology.

Sometime between now and Monday he was sure he would.

Okay, not sure.

Hopeful.

Okay, not all that hopeful.

Luke Miller was thoroughly and utterly lost. Dani meant more to him than Caitlyn ever had. More than any woman ever had. And there was a very good chance he'd blown it.

Dani realized that there is a certain terror that steals over you when you're about to go make a huge fool of yourself. But she steeled herself and walked into Chuckles anyway. She saw Allie and a crowd from work at one of the tables. She waved and they waved back.

After yesterday's meeting, things seemed to be much better on the work front.

The family front was great. The baby was beautiful and Mart had offered her another blind date. "Not that I think you'll keep it," he said. "But the three we've done together have turned out so good, friends are clamoring for a shot."

Yes, things were looking up.

Now, if only she could figure out her relationship with Luke.

She didn't see him anywhere, but did spot Sherri behind the bar.

"Hey, stranger," Sherri called when she spotted Dani. "I wasn't sure if we'd see you again after . . ." She let the sentence trail off.

"I wasn't sure you would either. But I'm here. Is Luke around, or is he hiding?"

"He wouldn't hide from you, Dani. He had to go out. He should be back soon."

"Okay, then."

"Are you going on?"

"Yes. Luke might have thought my attitude was unprofessional the other night, but the fact is, I'm not a professional. I'm an amateur who enjoys this as an avocation. He can't make me be something I'm not."

"I think you've got it all wrong. He doesn't want you to be anything but an amateur. But he sees the potential in you, just like I do. You have that innate sense of timing that comics need."

"But though I might play a comic on Thursday nights, I'm not. I publish books. I have no interest in going on a comedy tour. I want to stay here, build up Hamlin, be with my family and . . . with Luke, if he's interested."

"You two have a lot to talk about. But since he's not here, why don't you find a seat and take your turn center stage. You two can talk later."

"I have some friends here, as a matter of fact."

Sherri made a shooing motion. "Well, go join them then and I'll send him over when he arrives."

"Great." Okay, great was what she said, but great wasn't what she meant. What had she been thinking when she came up with this brilliant plan?

Einstein she wasn't.

She pushed back her fear of making a fool of herself and went to mingle with her coworkers and family. And as she moved from one group to another, she realized that no matter what, she was going to be okay. She had work on track, she had her family.

If she didn't have Luke . . .

No, she wasn't going to think like that.

"And now," Judy from WLVH called, "we have a woman who's become a crowd favorite in a very short time, Dani Sinclair, our own Corporate Comic."

As if on cue, Luke walked in. His head jerked up as he heard her name and he spotted her. For a moment, they just looked at each other. Dani felt a connection, but couldn't be sure if she was fooling herself or not. So, she gave him a small smile and wave, then headed up to the stage.

There, center stage, microphone in front of

her, and spotlight on her, her nerves finally calmed. "Thank you, Judy. Now, before I start tonight, I want to thank my coworkers for coming out and supporting me. And I want to thank them for being such great inspiration. Why, just the other day . . ."

She went off on the new bit she'd been playing with.

Greatest Office Hits, detailing in minute detail all the mishaps at Hamlin over the last few weeks. She kept looking at Allie's table, checking that no one was offended, and was relieved to see them all laughing at the appropriate places.

She fell into the rhythm, and was enjoying herself, but still, though they'd calmed, there was an undercurrent of nerves that had nothing to do with being on stage and everything to do with settling things with Luke.

He moved to the front of the room, stopping at an empty chair he sat, but his eyes never leaving her.

She stopped her bit mid-sentence. ". . . and the chair . . ."

Dani studied him, looking for some indication of how he was feeling. Was he happy to see her, or annoyed. She couldn't tell.

She knew she should wait, should talk to him

in private, but words started tumbling out of her mouth.

"Let's forget about my office mishaps and comedy bits. I want to talk about me. And regulars will know this isn't the first time my comedy routine has been less about comedy and more about me.

"I'm new to Erie. Well, not new. I grew up here, but I haven't lived here since I went off to college. I came home to be close to my family, and because I got offered a great new job. I didn't come here looking for a man. I don't have time for one.

"But there I was, my first day in town, jumping off a toilet and onto a bug, then running out of the bathroom when I literally bumped into a man. I hadn't even been looking, but there he was.

"Problem is, men are hard to figure out. I can plot a business plan, find and fix office problems, and I can spot an editorial mistake from five paces back. But men? I don't have a clue. Which is probably why I munged up this relationship with this really great man. After I'm done here tonight, I plan to talk to him, to see if there's anything I can do to salvage what we have, what we're growing into. Because I think it could be something special."

"Hey, you're not being very funny," Luke called from the audience.

"No heckling, please. This is a new autobiographic sketch I've been working on."

"Well, you've got it all wrong." He walked around the tables to the stairs stage left, and made his way to center stage.

"Here's how it should go. The other day I was standing on a toilet eyeing a bug. A killer-bug . . ." He looked at her and waited.

She took the cue. "You have to add the killer part, or it just sounds stupid."

He smiled and nodded approvingly. "Right. Then you should say, and when I jumped off the toilet and landed on the bug, ending it's killing spree, I opened the door and bumped into a gorgeous, handsome, intelligent—"

"How did I know he was intelligent?" Dani teased. "I'd just bumped into him?"

"Ah, you knew he was smart because he offered you a ride. He could see beyond your bug-gut covered shoes and your oh-so sensible suit. He could see beyond your bun and lack of makeup and recognize someone special."

"You know, I think your staff is right," Dani said, then tsked him. "You should stay off the stage, you're not very funny."

"But you like me anyway." He reached out and took her hand.

"Maybe a little."

"Maybe a lot."

"Yeah, maybe a lot," she admitted.

"Okay, since we've established I'm not funny, I'll let you finish your set, but I'd like to talk to you in private afterward."

"Oooooh," the audience said collectively, sounding just like kids in a class after someone gets called to the office.

Dani looked out and saw her mother shooting her a mom-eye and she knew what she had to do. "Listen, Luke, let's just cut to the chase. I like you. More than that, I love you. There I said. It's not funny, I'm not a professional comic. There it is."

"Well, it's not Shakespeare, that's for sure, but then, lucky for you, I don't need to be *Romeo'd*. I just need you." He pulled her close and whispered, "Me, too." Louder, so the audience could hear, he said, "For the record, I love Dani Sinclair."

"Kiss, kiss, kiss," the audience chanted.

Luke said, "Do you mind?"

Dani just laughed. "I thought you'd never ask."

From the Comedy Journals of Dani Sinclair:

So many women dream about the grandstand declaration, but the funny thing is, when it comes down to it, a simple, me, too is just as sweet as any Shakespearean son-net.

Chapter Fourteen
Final Bows

"Hi, this is Cassie Grant-Cooper here at WLVH, where love is more than just a song. And we've done it again. Oh, this time it wasn't a contest, and the relationship didn't include one of our employees . . . or two as the case may be. But we had our hand in this love match just the same. You see, WLVH partnered up with Chuckles comedy club, sending disc jockeys down to MC for them. And like magic, another romance happened between the club's owner and a certain new business woman with a penchant for stand-up and stand-up guys. Which is why I'm here, covering the wedding of Dani and Luke, another happy couple brought to you courtesy of WLVH.

"And in case you haven't heard, Dani, who

journaled her way to amateur stand-up fame, just announced her journal will be a book sometime next year. *The Orange Journal . . . A Comic Look at Love, Work and Life.*

"Books and comedy aside, here's the star. Dani is walking down the aisle on her father's arm. . . ."